THE BLUE BARON MYSTERY

Also By Jerry Labriola

—*The Saga of Hodge*
—*Murders at Hollings General*
—*Murders at Brent Institute*
—*The Maltese Murders*
—*The Strange Death of Napoleon Bonaparte*
—*Scent of Danger*
—*Object of Betrayal*
—*Deadly Politics*
—*Global Shadows*
—*Diamonds and Pirates*
—*Dangerous Triangle*

Coauthored with Dr. Henry Lee
—*Famous Crimes Revisited*
—*Forensic Files*
—*The Budapest Connection*
—*Shocking Cases*

THE BLUE BARON MYSTERY
A NOVEL
BY
JERRY LABRIOLA, M.D.

STRONG BOOKS

Strong Books
P.O. Box 1194
Middlebury, CT   06762

Copyright © 2017 by Jerry Labriola

ISBN 978-1-928-782-93-3
Paperback

Library of Congress Control Number: 2016952318
(Hardcover)

Published in the United States of America by Strong Books, an imprint of Publishing Directions, LLC

Printed in the United States of America

Dedicated to my wife, Lois, whose
meticulous reviews and inspiration helped
make this book possible

ACKNOWLEDGMENTS

My heartfelt thanks to the personnel at
Strong Books, especially Dan Uitti,
Brian Jud, Dan Zeno and Beth Bruno

NOTE

I have taken the liberty of presenting nearly
all dialogue in English to avoid the complexities
of multiple languages versus English.
J. L.

THE PLAYERS

Paul D'Arneau—treasure hunter and investigator who is hired to solve a mystery.

Sylvie D'Arneau—Paul's wife and an administrator at Cape Cod's Oceanographic Institute.

Leon Cassell—Chairman of *Gens de Vérité* who hired Paul.

Vincent Broussard—Paul's bodyguard and a Harvard professor.

Dennis Grabher—lead pilot for Paul's plane.

Otto Bleeker—Chief Commissioner of Amsterdam's police department.

George Webley—Otto's assistant police officer.

Fritz Van Camp—owner of an Amsterdam brewery.

Knute Larsen—prosecutor at The Hague.

Barry Burns—Captain of the Police League in Hyannis, Massachusetts.

Freda Hoek—spouse of a murder victim.

Guy Martin—Instructor of "Journalism and Communications" at Harvard.

Sophie Bauer—blood relative of Napoleon.

Joe Gomez—Police Chief of Buenos Aires.

Marlene Kessler—international prostitute.

Fabio Calderone—gang member from Italy.

Maurice Delacroix—expert on Napoleonic military history.

Catherina Frelinghuyens—spouse of murder victim.

Koenraad Mulder—brother of murder victim.

Basil Anagnos—Police Chief of Sarajevo.

Dora Adenovic—spouse of murder victim.

Al Rainford—Hyannis detective.

Stefan Weiss—head police officer at *Invalides*.

Chester Knight—assistant police officer at *Invalides*.

Juan Carlos Saltanban—Gibraltar communications expert.

PART ONE

PROLOGUE

It had happened to Paul D'Arneau before. While treasure hunting, having been hired to locate valuable family heirlooms, he would grow weary of dead-end challenges, subsidiary investigative work involving forensic details and, especially, international travel. Somehow, his body had conquered nearly all jet-lag consequences, no matter the distances involved: Argentina to Australia, Cape Horn to Siberia, Boston to Malasia. But time and again, the hours spent on airliners and cruise ships; on trains, buses and rented cars; even in negotiating highlands and wetlands on foot—all were taking their toll. He finally decided to take a breather and concentrate on a less demanding job as Chief Administrator of the Sterling Memorial Library at Yale University, but not for long.

The position was the remaining one in a list of those he'd held at his alma mater, from chairmanship of its history department to a much-in-demand lecturer on the History of the Early Modern Era. Along the way, he managed to author an historical textbook, a mystery novel and three books dealing with his longtime hero: *Napoleonic Strategy, Napoleon and Volterraio Castle,* and his recently completed, *Napoleon's Final Defeat*. All this in little more than three years.

The university had claimed that he'd become a "regressive mythologist" and an "obsessive and flamboyant admirer of the emperor." His termination notice stated that "Your most far-fetched theories about Napoleon's death and the scandalous side of his life are unacceptable improprieties against the chair you occupy and the faculty you represent."

He often spoke to himself about it. *A scholarship to this place. Decent grades. Wonderful years. Their hatred of Napoleon. The administration leaders here are **not** the university. Some of them are younger than I am.*

Not discouraged and unwilling to disassociate himself entirely from Yale, he turned to a former student roommate there—currently one of its largest financial contributors—and was put in charge of the library staff in short order. He was also granted "reasonable time off" to continue pursuit of his other passions: the aforementioned treasure hunting and two part-time activities—martial arts instructor and volunteering to rescue stranded mountain climbers on behalf of the Naval Investigative Service. The latter took place only during his 30s, however, because of time constraints.

Chapter 1

Early summer

A fter only four months, and without mixed feelings, Paul quit his job at Yale. He and his wife, Sylvie, moved from their Connecticut home to a large estate in Falmouth on Cape Cod. Surprisingly, they both hated leaving their prior grounds even more than the house. As a result they tried to mimic it in Falmouth and arranged for a regular gardener and arborist to maintain it in the same way. In front, a stone water fountain was installed along a sweep of ornamental grasses and purple-flowered Persian mint. And off to both sides were gardens containing shrubs with bright colored foliage and evergreens, while, in back, were plants of different sizes and shapes.

When they lived in Connecticut, Paul had round-the-clock security guards stationed—front

and back—for fear of retaliation by the Japanese
New Kamikazes and certain Somalian pirates
whose attempt to destroy the world with sarin gas
had been foiled by Paul. He'd furthermore taught
Sylvie how to use a revolver which she kept in her
purse. There had been no evidence of retaliation,
however, and he dispensed with guards in
Falmouth. *But was it the right decision?* There
were times at night when he heard strange noises
outside and, with loaded Beretta Cougar .45 in
hand, rushed out back to check. Or, instead, turning
on the outside lights, going to the nearest window
and peering out from beneath its shade. In every
instance, he had seen nothing remarkable.

As for Sylvie, after key administrative work
at the Academy of Sciences in Paris—where they
first met—she assumed the same type work at the
Cape's Woods Hole Oceanographic Institute.

Watching her prepare to leave for work on
this particular morning, he was on his second cup
of coffee, still in pajamas and slouched on the
Morris chair in his upstairs study. He thought she
looked her best in the morning, showing no signs
of sleep excess or deprivation; green eyes with a
summer sparkle no matter the season; raven hair,
every strand controlled; subdued scent of the
packaged fragrances he gave her every Christmas.
The fact that she—at five-feet-ten—was nearly as
tall as he mitigated against high heels, her Zara
ballet sandals or occasional flat ankle boots raising
her hardly at all. She once admitted that were she

shorter, she would feel less an equal during their rare disagreements.

"What's for today?" she asked.

"Nothing special for a change. You know my three R's: relaxing, resting and reading."

"I've thought of a fourth for you, my dear."

"What's that?"

"Recuperating."

"Recuperating from what?"

"From all the things that lead to your relaxing, resting and reading."

Neither one chose to exhaust the subject.

The enormous high-ceilinged study was once two bedrooms which Paul had morphed into what he now considered a "man cave and library" that was steeped in the past and much mimicked Winston Churchill's home with standing desk, a sixth-century Greek chair and a seventh-century Assyrian stool. Sylvie, however, called it his "Chest Room" for its score of chests—Italian, English, French, Egyptian—all dating back at least two-hundred years. But there were also numerous floor lamps, two foot-friendly coffee tables, a compact bar and wine cooler, a surround-sound system, a small TV screen, two computers, a printer, copying machine and other pieces of furniture. Paul spent hours there, if not writing at his beloved standing desk, just retreating to think. For this he seldom sat—especially if engaged in serious thought. For that he would pace for hours at

a time, just as he would in any surroundings—
karate studio, other homes, airports and the like.
But on rare occasions when he decided to sit, it was
in one of two recliners. He preferred the one made
of alligator leather because it reminded him of a
most successful assignment that required his
foraging a dirty brook with alligators lurking on
either side. One had lunged at him, but he delivered
a karate chop to just below its eyes, and it dragged
itself away.

Sylvie had long ago learned that these were
sessions in which he was not to be disturbed. And
she had long ago refrained from smiling during any
of his cracker munching, for the combination of
pacing and munching represented the most
menacing thoughts.

There was only one window in the room,
and Paul had made it so, for it allowed more wall
space for floor-to-ceiling shelves stuffed with
hundreds and hundreds of books, old and new.
Their topics ranged from astronomy to Zambia and
included a fair share of those dealing with
mythology, judo and, of course, Napoleon. There
were at least 20 about the emperor, including the
three he had authored himself. To reach the
uppermost shelves on the two longest walls, he had
installed sliding ladders that were replicas of the
numerous ones at the Sterling Library.

The breather lasted a mere three days when,
once again, he answered a phone call from Leon

Cassell, longtime Chairman of *Gens de Vérité*, a French organization that had been in existence since the fall of Napoleon Bonaparte in 1815. *Vérité* was a private group that worked alongside the French government but had never been part of it. When retained at a sizeable cost, it was noted for solving worldwide puzzles related to the national security and defense initiatives of countries that sought its help. Even to scientific issues that would impact specific countries. Within France, it took up causes as they developed, focusing on projects lacking any iota of political or special interest rhetoric. Membership extended throughout Europe and numbered about two-thousand.

　　With regard to Leon himself, he'd had a distinguished career in law enforcement. Early on, he was a captain of both the police force and the *Préfecture de Police* in Paris. Ten years later, he taught criminology at their *Grandes-Écoles* and, at the same time, lectured regularly at the Paris Police Museum. Currently he was teaching a course on Corrections, Crime and Criminology at what was once referred to as the Sorbonne and now as the University of Paris. Paul had many times heard Leon explain that it was ironic for the original College de Sorbonne to be suppressed during the French Revolution only to be reopened by Napoleon in 1808 and that today the university has many colleges. He would stress that the "Sorbonne" has become a colloquial term for the entire collection. Then too, he was proud of a strong relationship with the British military. Thus his background was full and varied. Paul had been called upon to lead several of *Vérité's* investigations and succeeded beyond expectations. Leon usually demanded more than Paul had been hired for, but Paul would remain tolerant because of Leon's relationship with Napoleon Bonaparte, a *blood* relationship based on DNA analysis. Paul had never inquired about such a connection either because he was doubtful of it or because it sounded too serious for a mind that felt cluttered most of the time. In such situations as this, he declared the subject insignificant. But it would later become extremely significant in the overall scheme of things and would have a direct and strong bearing on Paul's next move.

Several years before, there was a huge—and complicated—series of discussions between him and Leon. They revolved around a French statesman named Charles Talleyrand, a certain Lady Beckett, who was a top executive with the British East India Tea Company, and one Sophie Bauer, a spinster from Brussels who, it was alleged, also had a DNA-based relationship to Napoleon.

In the first place, it was generally accepted that Lady Beckett was one of Napoleon's lovers, even while he was exiled on St. Helena. And it appeared that through the influence of the tea company and with Talleyrand's manipulations, she managed to see Napoleon on a regular basis.

In the second place, no one was convinced that the emperor was later murdered; or that he had succumbed to cancer, as his father had; or that he died accidentally from arsenic inhaled from the colored wallpaper lining the walls of his sleeping quarters.

And in the third place, because of a poorly understood hypothesis, a possibility existed that Napoleon's body was not in a tomb at Paris' *Hôtel des Invalides* after all, but had been transferred to what was termed, "Beckett Gardens".

The upshot of it all was that Paul, his close friend Vincent, and Sylvie—his girlfriend at the time—went to the gardens, identified a resting place clearly identified as that of Beckett's lover, and dug down to a largely deteriorated coffin, some of it crumbled into dust.

Much of this was captured in Paul's most recent book, *Napoleon's Final Downfall:*

> Leon had arranged for a supervisor and three-man digging crew to accompany the trio to the gardens for an "inspection". The supervisor had raised questions about such a designation but was silenced and rewarded in no uncertain money terms.
>
> The cobblestone entry drive was bordered on both sides by stone pots on rock pedestals, pachysandra, rose geraniums, towering sycamores and plane trees. Far off

in the distance were row upon row of gravestones in a sea of yellows and reds and blues of early flowers that Paul couldn't identify. Fifty yards in, the supervisor pointed to Lady Beckett's headstone, off to the right. And it was there that Paul stated he wanted to begin their inspection. He urged the inspector to leave after assuring him that no defiling would take place, no damage done. The diggers, he said, would be used only to move away some earth in one or two areas suspected of housing old unmarked graves overgrown with vines or mixed vegetation.

Paul stood studying the area, then moved to a spot directly behind the headstone. In its shadow, the growth appeared thin, a fact other observers might have attributed to shielding of the sun by a ten-foot high marble slab. *But we're not looking for shallow headstones!*

He dug an inch into the ground with his foot. Two inches. More as the dirt seemed less compact. Then he met solid resistance.

"Here," he said to the diggers. "Could you please dig around here?"

They complied and within the length of a shovel blade, there was a clang. Paul had never conceived of trying to differentiate between the clang of metal on rock and the clang of metal on cement. But if he were now to place a wager, he would pick cement.

He felt the blotches come, asked the men to broaden the hole, grabbed a shovel excitedly from one of them and outlined a three-by-six-foot rectangular area around it. Before they had completely dug out the space, Paul looked at Sylvie and Vincent and shouted, "Pay dirt! Excuse the pun."

He kneeled down and cleaned off a one-foot square cement block with his hand. It bore an inscription in tiny letters:

WAIT FOR ME, MY BELOVED
IT WILL NOT BE LONG
1840

Paul's words came quickly now as did his movements, almost twitchy.

"The coffin there," he said, "can you—would you—open it? Your boss would give the go-ahead. I swear to it. I'll explain to him later."

The bulkiest of the diggers started in and the other two followed suit. They used tarnished tools taken from a tarnished toolbox. It didn't take long: iron screws dangled from the coffin's rim.

Paul and Sylvie's eyes stopped blinking as they beheld a mummified corpse before them. There were dirty cloth fragments over most of the wasted body ... yellowed ornaments, medals and two swords.

The corpse's skull had disarticulated from the rest of the body and lay at an awkward angle to the chest, the bones of which were riddled with pockmarks.

Silently, the three of them put on surgical gloves. Paul picked up the skull and with a penknife, scraped off a few bone fragments into a small glass container. He then carefully put them into his pocket, hoping they would yield some mitochondrial DNA, a type of genetic material he knew would not degrade for centuries. This in contrast to the usual nuclear DNA which degrades fairly rapidly. The only problem he could imagine in relying on the mitochondrial type is that it is passed on from generation to generation only in the female line of a family. Plus he knew that Napoleon had no female heirs except possibly a child he had fathered with Lady Beckett. Paul realized he was in the middle of a roll and, because of the thought of that child, that it bore an alarming resemblance to Huxley's *Brave New World* of children mechanically stratified and programmed.

This was neither of those, however, even though closer examination revealed a few grains of truth hidden in a sand pile of elaboration and unwarranted generalization. But that was the essence of his cerebral activity, and he let the roll continue with no intention of stopping it.

Whenever he thought of DNA, for example, he thought of genes. And whenever he thought of genes, he thought of having written about both hereditary elements in one of his books: "Genes are evolutionary glue, binding all life in a single history that dates back some 3.5 billion years—a history that is written in the language of nature's universal information molecule—DNA. It has certainly revolutionized forensic science—but we have to be very careful—because the information gleaned may not be the kind we'd want to share with everyone. People and institutions might, in fact, use it against you."

Paul could never recite such a paragraph word-for-word, but occasionally he'd render a quote for anyone who would listen. He was especially proud of "written in the language of nature's universal information molecule—DNA." And automatically, he equated DNA's being an information molecule with a definite possibility that the body was that of the great Napoleon.

Paul decided not to wait. He took out his cell phone and called Leon to pass on the news of their find. The reaction of *Vérité's* president was more evident in his voice than in his words: breathless, loud, raspier than usual. "I can't believe it," he said.

And Paul's voice was just as breathless. "There it is, Leon, right before us. An awful sight. An awful-looking casket, falling apart, the body deteriorated. Can we meet in the hotel lobby at about 7:30? I'll give you my theory about the background. For now I'll just say that the body was stolen in 1840 when it was supposed to be transferred to Paris. No doubt Lady Beckett was behind it. I see Talleyrand's hand in it too. She wanted Napoleon buried in her gardens and expected to join him there later. Now we have to prove it's definitely his body. The DNA business will take a few weeks in a case like this. Eventually, I'll work up a written report for you."

"My friend," Leon said this time around, "I know you need your rest, but if you're available, we need you. The membership is clamoring for you, I'm clamoring for you, and the whole world would be too—if only they knew what was at stake here.

And I promise—I won't go off expecting more than we'd initially agreed upon—if we agree at all."

Already, Paul was suspicious of the phraseology but decided to hear him out. "What's at stake?" he asked, sitting up. He'd been feeling awkward slouched in a chair, still in pajamas. "And would it by chance involve another lucrative assignment?"

A million here, a million there ... what the hell.

Somehow, it didn't fit with what he'd anticipated.

Leon continued: "Another assignment. Same arrangement. A million, plus expenses, including travel wherever it takes you. Lodging would be high quality and personal security would be provided if necessary. And if you agree, I wouldn't see the need for us to meet as we've usually done in the past. I'll just email you with more background or to alert you of any new developments. That doesn't mean we shouldn't meet at all, just less often."

"Or phone me—and vice-versa."

"Hmm, sounds like you're already interested."

Paul had received the same kind of talk before and decided to tone down his remarks until he received the full details. "Sorry," he said. "I'd better keep my trap shut while you just go ahead.

I'm willing to listen and will give you a yes-or-no as soon as you finish. Fair enough?"

"Fair enough. And I don't think you have to consult the same fellows you usually do here in Paris, mainly because I don't think they have the experience with most of what I'm about to say."

"Unless Napoleon comes into the picture— right?"

"Right, and he does. Very much so. Not in terms of what he accomplished as a military man, but in terms of some people mentioning his name without knowing the deadly consequences they'd face."

"Mentioning his name? But so what? What does that do to those people?"

"Kills them."

Paul had trouble processing what he'd just heard and became as tense as a spring, for what to him had begun pretty much as word salad had suddenly drifted into something worth hunting down. As dangerous as it sounded.

"Incredible!" he said, "but let me say then … two things … first, that I'm halfway to saying yes … and second, that some of my friends kid me about claiming I know more about Napoleon than did any of his wives and lovers. Do you know anything about them?"

"For sure."

Paul heard loud paper rattling at the other end and was certain that Leon was putting some notes in order. In fact, he indicated that was exactly what he was doing—arranging notes and even lining up some books—and apologized for a most pregnant pause in their conversation. "You've got time to listen to some of this?" he asked.

"About Napoleon? All the time you need."

"Well, many, many women made him happy. Two he married, others were mistresses and they lived all over the map: Josephine, Marie Louise, Désirée, Pauline, Marie Walewska, Mademoiselle Georges, Giuseppina, Madame de Stael. He liked to flaunt his mistresses but once said, 'I am not a man like others and moral laws or the laws that govern conventional behavior do not apply to me. My mistresses do not in the least engage my feelings. Power is my mistress.' But he wrote love letters to all of them and each one sounded more convincing than the others."

Paul was in another world as he asked, "And about his time at St. Helena—when he was away from all his women—what did he do with his time there besides what we've all read about? You know … like walking, gardening, billiards, cards, chess, dictating memoirs?"

"Apparently Lady Beckett was regularly sneaked in, but for the conqueror of most of Europe, nearly six years in captivity must have been pure hell. He was miserable. It says as much over and over again in all the books I've read about him. He was miserable, I repeat, and he became melancholic. He evidently just sat a lot, staring off

into space. Some experts think he was turning
schizophrenic—even before he abdicated—before
St. Helena. And there are some hints that as time
wore on, he began suffering from some kind of
paranoia. I have a collection of entries to his diary,
Paul, and I'd like to read some to you. Two that
probably address his mental state; four that are
examples of his love letters; and a last one that is
most revealing. Most revealing! You be the judge.
It'll take a while, but I think it's worth it because it
sheds light on his mental state and even, when he
talks about his conquests in the last entry, you can
get a sense of the enormity of it all. Keep in mind
that it's hard to tell when changes in his mental
state began—during his last military defeats or
once he was settled in on that island. You game for
me to continue?"

"Please do. I'm all ears."

"And when I get to his love letters, do notice
the choice of words, the flow of his sentences, the
contradictory nature of expression to separate
women.

"First, we have: *A questa Casa. O in questo
luogo tristo, non voglio niente di lu:*

> I hate this Longwood House. The
> sight of it makes me melancholy. Let them
> put me in some place where there is shade,
> verdure, and water. Here it either blows a
> furious wind, loaded with rain and fog, *chi*

mi taglia l'anima; or if that is wanting, *il sole mi brucia il cervello*, through the want of shade when I go out.

"I think the importance of this one, Paul, is the use of Italian rather than French. He was born on an Italian island, remember—Corsica—and he didn't move to France until he was in his early 20's. So is what I just read a sign of abnormal regression ... back to his childhood?

"As for a second entry, I'm no psychiatrist but it strikes me as weird—very weird:"

Man loves the supernatural; he meets deception halfway. The fact is that everything about us is a miracle. Strictly speaking, there are no phenomena, for in nature everything is a phenomenon: my existence is a phenomenon; this log that is being put in the chimney is a phenomenon; my intelligence, my faculties, are phenomena; for they all exist, yet we cannot define them. I leave you here, and I am in Paris, entering the opera; I bow to the spectators, I hear the acclamations, I see the actors, I hear the music. Now if I can span the space from St. Helena, why not that of the centuries? Why should I not see the future as the past? Would the one be more extraordinary, more marvelous than the other? No, but in fact it is not so.

"And the initial love letter is to Josephine, the first of his two wives. She was unable to give him children, so he divorced her in 1810."

> I have not spent a day without loving you; I have not spent a night without embracing you; I have not so much as drunk a single cup of tea without cursing the pride and ambition that force me to remain separated from the moving spirit of my life. In the midst of my duties, whether I am at the head of my army or inspecting the camps, my beloved Josephine stands alone in my heart. Occupies my mind, fills my thoughts. If I am moving away from you with the speed of the Rhone current, it is only that I may see you again more quickly. If I rise to work in the middle of the night, it is because this may hasten by a matter of days the arrival of my sweet love. Josephine! Josephine! Remember what I have sometimes said to you: Nature has endowed me with a virile and decisive character. It has built yours out of lace and gossamer.

"The second love letter is to his second wife, Marie-Louise, Archduchess of Austria and later Empress of the French. Note that he doesn't refer to love until the very end:"

> To Marie-Louise: You have sent me a very beautiful comfit box with the portrait of the King of Rome at prayer. I want you to have it engraved with the caption: "I pray to God to save my father and France." This little picture is so interesting that it will please everybody. I am sending you Mortemarte with 20 flags captured from the Russians, the Prussians and the Austrians. My health is good. The Emperors of Russia and Austria, and the King of Prussia were at Pont, at Madame's; they went there from Bray, and their headquarters were to have been at Fontainebleau on the 18th. They are now making post-hast for Troyes. My troops have entered Nogent and Sens. Give my son a kiss, keep well, and never doubt my love.

"The third—probably the longest—is to Marie Walewska:"

> I saw no one but you, I admired no one but you, I want no one but you. Answer me at once, and assuage the impatient passion of N. Ah! Grant a few moment's

pleasure and happiness to a poor heart that is
only waiting to adore you. Is it so difficult to
let me have an answer? You owe me two.
There are times—I am passing through one
now—when hope is as heavy as despair.
What can satisfy the needs of a smitten
heart, which longs to throw itself at your
feet, but is held back by the weight of
serious considerations, paralyzing its
keenest desires. Oh, if only you would! No
one but you can remove the obstacles that
keep us apart. Marie, my sweet Marie, my
first thought is of you, my first desire is to
see you again. I want you to accept this
bouquet. I want it to be a secret link, setting
up a private understanding between us in the
midst of the surrounding crowd. We shall be
able to share our thoughts, though all the
world is looking on. When my hand presses
my heart, you will know that I am thinking
of no one but you. And when I press your
bouquet, I shall have your answer back!
Love me, my pretty one, and hold your
bouquet tight.

"The fourth was to Lady Beckett and
it read:"

You have made my last years
tolerable, even more so than during the
several before when I expended my full

energy upholding the desires of many in the battlefield. And now I must fritter away the minutes, my heart, my soul trapped here until you steal to me once more. I await that time with more impatience than you could ever know, my darling. Your smile and golden locks fill my waking hours. I feel strange and weakened but he would be a fool who turned away from the inevitable. The Valley of Geraniums would be my choice if I could not but have my final resting place in your English gardens, beside you for an eternity.

"But the last entry in his diary is exceptional—in more ways than one. What would you call it in America? A doozie? The clincher of all clinchers? The words convey such scope, such grandeur, but they can also be the words of a paranoid. He was always prone to grandiose proclamations, but none like these. Notice his referral to himself not as 'I' or 'me', but as 'Napoleon'. And the tone of the boasting has meaning. Granted it was no doubt directed against those who would defame him, but I think there's a possibility, even a probability, that the guy was completely mad. Nuts. He wrote this in the ninth month of his confinement so I have to ask once again: Was he already deteriorating when he arrived and, if so, was it because of military defeats or because of arsenic? This is what he wrote. It's long and tedious, but it's revealing—almost like a history lesson:"

You want to know the treasures of Napoleon? They are enormous, it is true, but in full view. Here they are: the splendid harbor of Antwerp, that of Flushing, capable of holding the largest fleets; the docks and dykes of Dunkirk, of Havre, of Nice; the gigantic harbor of Cherbourg; the harbor works in Venice; the great roads from Antwerp to Amsterdam, from Mainz to Metz, from Bordeaux to Bayonne; the passes of the Simplon, of Mont Cenis, of Mont Genevre, of the Corniche that gave four openings through the Alps; in that alone you might think 800 millions. The roads from the Pyrenees to the Alps, from Parma to Spezzia, from Savona to Piedmont; the bridges of Jena, of Austerlitz, of the Arts, of *Sèvres*, of Tours, of Lyons, of Turin, of the *Isère*, of the Durance, of Bordeaux, of Rouen; the canal from the Rhine to the Rhone, joining the waters of Holland to the Mediterranean; the canal that joins the Scheldt and the Somme, connecting Amsterdam and Paris; that which joins the Rance and the Vilaine; the canal of Arles, of Pavia, of the Rhine; the draining of the marshes of Bourgoing, of the Citentin, of Rochefort; the rebuilding of most of the churches pulled down during the Revolution, the building of new ones; the construction of many industrial establishments for putting an end to pauperism; the construction of the Louvre, of the public graneries, of the Bank, of the canal of Ourcq; the water system of the city of Paris, the numerous sewers, the quays, the embellishments and monuments of the great city; the public improvements of Rome; the reestablishment of the manufactories of Lyons. Fifty million spent on repairing and improving the Crown residences; sixty million worth of furniture placed in the palaces of France and Holland, at Turin, at Rome; sixty million worth of Crown diamonds, all of it the money of Napoleon; even the Regent, the only missing one of the old diamonds of the Crown of France, purchased from Berlin Jews with whom it was pledged for three millions; the Napoleon museum, valued at more than 400 millions. These are monuments to confound calumny. History will relate that all of this was accomplished in the midst of continuous wars, without raising a loan, and with the public debt actually decreasing by the day.

"So what do you think, Paul?"

"Sounds like Napoleon is more important than anything else in this assignment."

"No, I don't mean it to be, but he's important in two out of the three components of it."

"Not that I'm complaining, understand. He's what actually might seal the deal."

"The deal?"

"Yeah, my accepting the assignment."

An unusually long pause ensued, which Paul interpreted as Leon's getting more notes in order. Finally, he said, "You know, I've rambled enough so I'll get started on the assignment. This will be as concise as I can make it, and what I don't cover now I'll cover by email. That is, if you agree to accept. And if you do, you'll get the email in about an hour. But I must level with you in advance. It will sound like a straightforward challenge but it's not. It's thorny—involving diamonds and other precious stones, but also murders, wars, history and such. You'd definitely have your hands full, but if anyone can put it all together, it's you. So I do hope you'll take it on."

No doubt he was referring to what he'd always thought of Paul: that he was as skilled in reducing a set of problems into a single solution as he was in taking a series of solutions and combining them into a single but complex thought. Never equivocating, never backing off. Years of collaboration had led Leon to such an appraisal.

Paul remained silent until Leon said he hoped Paul would take the case.

"I need to hear more, Leon."

"That's where my email comes in."

At this juncture, Paul slipped over to the desk and readied his notepad. "Okay," he said, "but maybe you can give me a bit of a preview. I'll be writing it down."

"Fair enough. And less for me to email. I'll make a few points. They're related but bear with me. First, you've heard of 'blood diamonds'?"

"Of *what*?"

"I take it you haven't. Well, they're also called 'hot diamonds', 'conflict diamonds' or 'war diamonds'. They're terms used for diamonds mined in a war zone and sold to finance an insurgent or invading army's war efforts or a warlord's activity. They pertain, for example, to diamonds mined during fairly recent wars in Angola, Belgium and Sierra Leone. Take Angola, for example. In the late '90s, it sold diamonds to finance a war with its own government. And that's the kind of thing that happened during civil wars in these and other African countries. Diamonds intensified civil wars by financing militaries and rebel militias. As recently as 2013, a civil war erupted in the Central African Republic with both sides fighting over the country's diamond resources. Thousands of people died and more than a million were displaced. Past wars fueled by diamond considerations have taken almost four million lives. In fact, millions of people are still dealing with the consequences of wars like that: friends and family members lost, lives shattered, physical and emotional scars that will last for generations. It's a nightmare and diamonds are in the middle of it.

"Secondly, there's a very famous diamond that was stolen. It's called the 'Blue Baron', originated in Amsterdam, and was modeled after the legendary Hope Diamond now housed in your Smithsonian Institution. They say the Blue Baron's value was set at $80,000 per carat but no one's sure how big it is. Some believe it's cursed and the reason is simply this: anyone who publicly announces they want to purchase it and also mentions—are you ready for this?—Napoleon's name at the same time—well, that person is murdered!"

Paul's pencil ran off the page when he heard the last statement.

"And my final point is that six people have been murdered, including two who are members of *Vérité*. Both lived in Amsterdam. One's a woman: Annie Snider. The other's Johan Wannamaker. We often contacted each other on many, many things. I can't believe they're gone."

Paul had scribbled down a half page of notes. He then twisted the headpiece of his phone and momentarily stared at it as if it were Leon. "But wait a second," Paul said, "I have some points of my own—questions really. Why didn't those jerko countries deal in real money, not diamonds?"

"I'm not sure. Ancient tradition, I guess."

"How long have the murders been going on?"

"About six weeks, as I understand it. The new Blue Baron is key in all of this and my colleagues believe that there's only one killer involved. We have an official informant who believes the same thing, so we're proceeding on that supposition. I, myself, don't understand why he couldn't have some kind of accomplice—or maybe two. But regardless, he … or they … are trying to locate the one and only new diamond, and he … or they … are committing murders to do so."

"Wait, Leon. Let's back up. Wouldn't one or two murders have raised suspicion earlier than now?"

"The pattern didn't become obvious until murder number six."

"The Napoleon connection must be a real stickler after all these years," Paul said. "And the other stickler is: if I go ahead and accept your offer, what does it entail anyway?"

He braced himself for the kind of answer he expected, for he was used to receiving tailored responses from Leon whenever the subject matter was weighty and/or conclusive.

"Find the killer to stop the murders. Locate the Blue Baron as help."

Weighty. Conclusive.

"And how does Napoleon fit in, other than the mention of his name?"

"I'll elaborate in my email. For now I'll say he, or at least the area around his sarcophagus in Paris, will become important. Very."

"I accept the assignment."

Without doubt, the Napoleon issue was the deciding factor. Paul swallowed deep in his throat, for he wasn't convinced who was more relieved that a definite decision had been reached. Even as he'd held impatience in check while listening to a barrage of love letters and braggadocio a la a sick Napoleon. And he could picture Leon jumping for joy as he heard him say: "Thank you so much, Paul. That's settled. You know, if you were female and I were there now, I'd kiss you."

"You're age what? Sixty-seven? It would be the first time I'd levy a jujitsu move on a guy 20 years my senior," Paul said, his tone unmistakably jovial.

Leon offered no response but moved to advice he'd given Paul during past crises. "Once again I'll throw in that those historian friends of yours may need to be consulted."

"Not *historian*, Leon—*histarian*. And of course I plan to. As you know, I'm one myself and we, as a group, make it easier for one another ... scattered around as we are."

"So maybe you should visit Amsterdam first and determine what you can regarding the *Vérité* murders. Is one of your histarians there?"

"More than one actually, but the one I've often worked with is Fritz Van Camp. He runs a top notch brewery there."

"Well, that's the way to begin, I would think. They've helped out so much in our other cases together. I should know by now, but tell me about them again."

"Glad to." Paul then unfolded a card from the wallet in his back pocket and, as he had done for many clients before, read what he had compiled some time ago:

> Histarians are individuals, male or female, who are located in practically every region of the civilized world and can provide information that cannot be gotten any other way. Very few people know of their existence. They give out facts only to other histarians or to those who come highly recommended. Very often they provide insights that are contrary to what history has recorded, so they are properly named. Not "contrarians" but "histarians".
>
> Most of them like to remain anonymous. They never offer a definitive opinion without first checking with others of their kind … they are constantly doing so … that is checking or verifying … in addition to delving into things with their own critical eye.

Some who have heard of them claim they possess mystical powers, but they have nothing of the sort. They simply do exhaustive research ... "private collections from private collectors" they call it. Their information sources are never revealed, but their conclusions always turn out to be right. It's superfluous to say ... but totally right and totally accurate. And they act fast, providing answers within a day or two.

They have sort of a code they live by ... "canon" might be a better word: "Never release information unless you'd die over its accuracy." So they rely on solid facts, not on opinion alone ... although they will express an opinion of other histarians, usually more than three or four. Four is the general rule.

Finally, they rarely give out much by telephone or over the Internet ... only in person.

"There," Paul said. "I've recited it so many times, I practically know it by heart."

"You know you have them to turn to—that's the important part."

"Yeah, I agree. Alright ... so we begin another experience together. Do email me with more information. I'll be waiting, or *we'll* be waiting. I'm asking Vincent to come with me. You remember him, I'm sure."

"Broussard? I certainly do. He'll be excellent … and he's trustworthy."

"Plus courageous. He's teaching at Harvard now, but I'm certain he can arrange for some time off. And one last thing, Leon."

"What's that?"

Paul crossed his fingers. "How much time do I have to accomplish everything?"

"As much as you need … or want."

"Well, just so you know … I'm not rushing. I'm changing my tempo. That, or I'll become a basket case."

"I understand. Take your time."

They terminated the phone call and Paul, surprised that his weariness was nearly gone, sat back and, typically, envisioned a list of things that had to be faced: shower and shave; notify Sylvie; call Harvard; arrange air travel; call Fritz. Most were routine but not his phoning Fritz, never considering a talk with that particular histarian even close to that. He believed all could be done before the email arrived an hour from then, even while expending additional time reliving the latest example of Vincent's courage. Having referred to the subject with Leon prompted Paul's train of thought. The example took place six months before. The location was on the island of Elba— site of Napoleon's first exile—just below the island's guardian, Volterraio Castle. Again working for *Vérité*, they were there to enter the castle, hoping to find information about whether or not the emperor had been murdered. Paul could still picture what took place, but he sensed it would prove to be more vivid were he to read about it in one of his published books, *Napoleon and Volterraio Castle*. He pulled down one of several copies from the nearest bookshelf and located the appropriate pages within seconds. He scanned them at first and was astounded at what he'd recalled when he wrote the book. *Had to be approximations, right? Especially the dialogue.* He then proceeded to read the following:

> The castle was perched on the summit of a rocky cliff that amounted to a collection of massive boulders with no paths to climb, nor any shrubs to grab onto during an ascent. Paul, Vincent and Sylvie hardly spoke during the 15-minute drive to the "rutted road". Vincent stopped the car and all three piled out. Sylvie began taking pictures. From their vantage point, the castle was more imposing than Paul had anticipated. He thought it bizarre that the only vegetation was either dotted around their shoes or, as viewed against the morning's darkening clouds, clinging to the castle itself. Isolated blades of yellow grass brushed against Paul's ankles while the castle itself appeared smothered in green, brown and yellow, like a camouflaged

fortress. He knew its construction dated back to the 11th century's Pisan period and that it had no doubt shrunk in size. Still it appeared indestructible to him and there were other words that swept through his mind: powerful, graceful, dignified. Most of all: timeless.

He hadn't discussed it with the others but Paul had every intention of inspecting the castle up close, to glance over an entire sea as the Tuscans had done to spot invading Saracen pirates; to see its underground tunnels firsthand; to walk along its walls much like Napoleon had two centuries ago, before the crumbling and erosion had begun. He also wanted to observe the blackbirds he'd read about. They had been delivered there as a trick, and he understood their offspring still nested among the ruins. In the dim light, he could barely make out a few circling about. Theirs were the only sounds he heard. Much smaller than normal, they gave the illusion that the structure was bigger than it was, as viewed from far off by the French, the Turks, the Saracens or any other enemies. And who knows, he mused, perhaps they might stumble upon something left behind, something hidden centuries before and now exposed. The box that Napoleon allegedly carried on his frequent visits there? *And if so, what was in it?*

He removed his sunglasses for it was growing darker by the minute. He then asked Sylvie to wait in the car and lock its doors.

"You ready?" he whispered to Vincent.

"If you are. What looks like a route to the top?"

Paul tweaked his chin. "Let's check around," he said. "You go that way and I'll go the opposite." He pointed to his left and right. "If you find a halfway decent approach, give me a holler, but not too loud. I'll do the same."

"Got it," Vincent said. "Incidentally, why are we speaking so softly?"

"So we might hear echoes of Napoleon's voice. The rumor is that he routinely spoke out loud in Italian up there."

They both chuckled. As Vincent went off, Paul circled to the right. He passed giant rock after giant rock on his left side. Interspersed among them were formations that brought to mind the stalagmites of caves he had explored such as those in the Rock of Gibraltar. He stopped occasionally to survey possible routes to the castle up high and, after a bend in the road, he looked back and saw that their car was no longer visible. Up ahead, several boulders formed a mound nearer the gutted road, narrowing it some.

What the!

Paul thought his heart would race out of control.

Twenty yards in front of him, he saw three men leaning against the back of a black sedan. They straightened in unison, hands on hips, legs apart. Red hoods covered their heads. The eye and mouth slots were overly large, revealing dark skin and mustaches. All three moved slowly toward him.

What to do? Strike up a conversation? Say, "Excuse me?" He might have done so had they not been wearing hoods.

Suddenly he heard Vincent's voice from behind and slightly hillside. He held a pistol in each hand. "Back off!" he screamed at the men. He leaped onto the road and swiftly positioned himself in front of Paul.

The men kept coming.

"Stop or else! I mean it!" Vincent's voice was louder and firmer as he straightened both arms toward the hooded men, now ten yards away.

They stopped.

"Put your hands behind your head, all of you." Without taking his eyes off them,

Vincent twisted his mouth to the side and said, "Show 'em, Paul, in case they don't understand."

Paul complied and the men followed suit.

"Now, one by one, take out your guns—I'm sure you have some—and throw them on the ground," Vincent continued. "And don't try anything funny. I've shot these pistols many times before. Shake your heads if you understand me."

They shook their heads and within seconds, five handguns lay on the road.

"You in the middle," Vincent said, "only one gun?"

The man didn't respond. Vincent tipped his pistol in his direction and the man reached into his back pocket.

"Easy now," Vincent said. The man flipped a small pearl-handled gun onto the road.

"Thank you, gentlemen. Now all of you—on the ground, face down, hands behind your head."

They spoke for the first time, each saying, "Si."

Vincent handed one of the guns to Paul and said, "Keep them covered. Every second." He picked up the guns and hurled them far up the cliff, one at a time. He then walked over to their sedan and shot out its tires. "Let's go," Vincent said. "There's enough room to turn our car around. And you guys? We're walking backwards, so don't dare get up until we're out of sight. Get it?"

As they inched away, Paul remained stunned over Vincent's skill in taking control of the situation.

"Why didn't you whisper to me that you'd be doubling back?" he asked.

"Because I figured if we were somehow being watched, he or they would notice that I didn't want them to. Besides, it wasn't necessary for you to know."

At the car, Sylvie bolted out. "I was so worried. I didn't know what to do. There were four shots. What happened?"

"Nothing," Vincent said. "Just testing my pistol."

They got into the car, Sylvie in back. Vincent maneuvered the car around and they sped off through a heavy but fleeting rain. It reminded Paul of his boyhood vacations in Florida.

"So you carry a gun, Vincent?" Sylvie asked in disbelief.

"Around here? For sure."

"Back in Paris, you don't seem like the gun type."

"But away from Paris, I can even swallow swords."

"If you don't mind, let's level with her," Paul chimed in.

Vincent's expression didn't register disapproval and Paul explained what had transpired, ending with, "Let's get out of here fast and I don't mean this place. I mean the whole damn island. Screw it!"

In the hotel lobby, the conversation was totally one-sided. Paul's precise words gushed out as if he couldn't wait to get rid of them, and Vincent nodded over and over.

"When I took on this assignment," Paul said, "I never bargained for this kind of stuff. I've hunted for lost treasures all over the world—six continents—and never faced this. I'm calling Leon. Let's see when the plane can get here."

Paul had no comment when Leon had said the challenge would be to "find the killer and therefore stop the murders. *Maybe locating the Blue Baron would do the same thing.*" He could understand the part about finding the killer, but the role of a stolen new diamond remained a puzzle.

Chapter 2

A fter showering and shaving, all signs of Paul's weariness had disappeared. Indeed, he felt energized and ready for action. Uncharacteristically, he had paused to view himself ... naked ... in the full-length mirror just beyond the shower stall. At age 50, what he saw was a six-foot tall man still fit to tackle whatever lay ahead. Trim, yet broad-shouldered and muscular, his wavy dark hair and penetrating brown eyes stood out, and he looked around before practicing a well-known ready smile. All in all, he felt reassured in observing little if any change in the past ten years.

Next was the call to Sylvie. He might have waited until she returned from work but was overly anxious to inform her of his acceptance.

"I could have predicted it," she said evenly.

"How so?"

"You can't sit still for longer than a day or two. Never have."

"As usual, you're right on the button."

"Anyway, darling, I applaud you and I applaud the million dollars."

"Oh? Which do you applaud more?"

Sylvie gave no reply.

"So?"

"I'm thinking; I'm thinking."

"You sound like Jack Benny, you know. And incidentally, I won't call you after I get the email. It can wait till you get home."

The next call was to Vincent. Paul had expected to encounter a considerable number of questions, but the Harvard professor limited them to a few after assuring Paul he'd accompany him throughout the following weeks.

"Where are we heading for starters?" Vincent had asked.

"Amsterdam. And the other places will depend on what we find out as we go along. Right now the whole assignment is kinda fuzzy, but we've had fuzzier ones before."

Paul had a sudden but fleeting urge to call the whole thing off, but he didn't let on, instead putting forth his usual stalwart facade at the start of any mission that seemed too vague to undertake. A measure of energy had been replaced by a measure of distress.

"We'll have our regular histarian helpers?" Vincent asked.

"What? Say it again."

"We'll have our regular historian helpers?"

"Oh yeah. In Amsterdam, it's Fritz Van Camp. Remember him?"

"Absolutely. How can I forget? Good—I feel better already. And the airport we leave from—the same?"

"The same. Not the Royal Air Force out of London but the Joint Base Cape Cod right here on the Cape … JBCC of Hyannis."

"So I can bring my gun?"

"Yes, sir."

Paul had done some investigative work for the base, home to four military command units that train for airborne search and rescue operations at home and abroad. His reward was two-fold: one, their availability for flight on a moment's notice. Anywhere. Anytime. For as long as necessary. That meant one of its smaller planes manned by two pilot friends would remain at a particular destination, awaiting Paul's request to continue on elsewhere. They would even dispatch a limo to and from his Falmouth home whenever necessary. And two, a mutual agreement not to disclose that he and any companion were allowed to be armed with a gun or guns while in flight. Paul was usually armed with a loaded Beretta Cougar .45 in a left shoulder holster and a Heritage Stealth 9 mm in a right ankle rig. Paul never asked why a JBCC plane was never searched, nor a landing ever "logged in" at any destination.

Vincent agreed to meet him at the Cape Cod airport at eight the next morning, covering the drive from Cambridge to Hyannis—down routes three and six— in little more than an hour. He would leave his car at one of the airport's secluded area.

Paul's last phone conversation was with Fritz, the histarian, who once again extended an eager and unequivocal desire to help out. After Paul had outlined the nature of the task at hand, Fritz asked him to phone the brewery or his home upon arrival. He also commented on the difficulty of the task.

"I know," Paul responded. He hoped to put forth a masking of his distress by adding, "but an old football coach, Vince Lombardi, once said, "The man on the top of the mountain didn't fall there."

Leon's email arrived at eleven-fifteen a.m. Paul read through it twice, taking notes, making faces—at once amorphous and quizzical— eyebrows raised.

> Paul: I've explained what war diamonds are. And regarding the stolen Blue Baron diamond: is it a replica of the famous Hope Diamond? We know where the latter is (Smithsonian) but where is the former?

Somebody must have it and the killer desperately wants it.

I've mentioned certain countries to you and I believe that you must visit some or all of them. The Netherlands is obvious, but I also suggest Angola, Belgium and Sierra Leone. Your histarian friends can help you decide. The last three have had internal wars during which diamonds have played significant roles in financing them. The Blue Baron is the one single item that can deter future wars against or within a nation, so the nation might be protected for years to come. Each of them has implied that it has the patience to wait and see if it can secure such a diamond. If it does, it can then announce, "Do not attack us and we will give you the diamond." But is there any other reason why each would want it? **YES**. If it advertises such an ownership, it improves its overall gemstone exchange. That is, its diamond wholesale exchange— its business of supplying large amounts of cut and polished diamonds throughout the world.

Now for Napoleon. The area around his sarcophagus may be important to check out. It involves a picture. Of what and exactly where, I can't say—because I don't know. What I can say is that one of my trusted British military friends received an anonymous letter referring to it. He knew of my interest in all of this and passed on the information to me.

That's it for now. Carry on and good luck. Call if you feel the need. Leon

Paul immediately sent back an email of thanks and indicated that he and Vincent would leave for Amsterdam early the next morning.

PART TWO

Chapter 3

O n the eight-hour flight and for the first time, Paul couldn't be sure, but he believed his outright worry about or disregard of jet lag had something to do with an automatic sleep reflex. He fought hard to postpone shutting his eyes for there were so many thoughts creeping around in his head. He was reminded of the many hours learning the jujitsu moves that he would not only teach others but that had served him well in his many international encounters. He referred to them as his "Trade Away From Home."

Away from home? My work is mostly overseas.

It had become a ritual while cramming his suitcase in the overhead bin (keeping a stuffed satchel at his feet) for he had to hold such martial arts moves at the ready and, early on, also in abeyance. All other thoughts continued to creep, however—interrupting a steady sleep—for what he would be doing, saying and arranging. Even where they would be taking place was an impenetrable mystery. He let it be this time around, counseling himself against trying to imagine any and all possibilities. He felt secure, however, in having Vincent along, one he judged to be a perfect bodyguard. And he looked the part too, hardly that of a young college professor, rather a boxer or wrestler, anyone with broad shoulders nearly matching Paul's. They always complemented one another, so much so that Paul felt it was destiny's work in pairing them during all past callings.

The plane touched down at the Schiphol Airport just before 2 p.m. that day, a Thursday. It jockeyed over to a deserted side area and came to a halt. Then the lead pilot and longtime friend, Dennis Grabher, approached Paul and Vincent.

"Sorry we haven't talked much," Dennis said, "but the most important question is: How was the flight?"

"Excellent," Paul replied, "as always. I think you make wind currents cringe."

"And you and Vincent have been well?"

"As well as could be expected," Vincent said judiciously.

They retrieved their luggage and sauntered forward toward the cockpit. Paul waved to the other pilot who was fiddling with a flight log. And before deplaning, Paul turned back to Dennis and said, "Don't know exactly where we're heading— though the police department's first—but I'll be phoning you. Your smartphone number hasn't changed?"

"No, and take your time, Paul. I know your job can get complicated. Just phone me when you're ready to move on. And don't forget: we can arrange for a helicopter if you need one." Dennis then said he'd summon a cab for them. "You're staying at the same hotel?" he asked.

"Yeah, the Schiphol, but I'd like to begin with the local police department."

He phoned ahead and learned that Otto Bleeker, the Chief Commissioner, would be glad to see him again. They had worked together on several past cases. "I started a police procedural for you again," the chief said. "It summarizes what we've accumulated thus far, and I know you like them."

On other trips to Amsterdam, Paul always spent the first half of the 20-minute drive from airport to hotel gazing out the taxi's back window, mesmerized by what he beheld and often by what he never had an opportunity to behold but still imagined: a capitol city featuring a concentric network of canals spanned by an estimated 400 bridges, all told. He'd crossed only a couple dozen or so and found they resembled one another. As did the numerous bicycles—driven or chained to posts or metal railings. Cycling was a popular mode of transportation in this city and surrounding flat regions. But what always intrigued him the most were the rows upon rows of city houses that dated back 300 years ... narrow-fronted, ornamented by triangular gables and superbly maintained in traditional Dutch fashion. As were famed rows of tulips that ranged in color from brilliant red to vivid orange to soft pink and apricot.

He usually passed the last half of the trip with reading, and his favorite subject always wound up being Napoleon Bonaparte. As one who had digested nearly everything about him, his continued reading was repetitious, but Paul didn't mind. Were one to comment on the behavior— Sylvie, for example—she characterized it as an obsession, similar to his pacing and munching crackers. Paul dug into his satchel and withdrew a collection of articles about his "hero". He perused them all, pausing and reflecting on each subject as if he wished to solidify what he already knew about it: the rise to power; the victories; the defeats; months at Waterloo; love affairs; years at St. Helena; conflicts with Charles Maurice de Talleyrand; Lady Beckett and the East India Tea Company; the arsenic theories; his military strategies, some of which current-day experts consider still viable.

In the windowless office of the Hoofdcommissaris or Chief Commissioner, Paul and Vincent were asked to make themselves comfortable in padded chairs, the only things comfortable-looking in a large and nearly vacant room. It looked like a place hardly ever occupied, leading Paul to believe it was more like a conference room than an office, especially for the head of Amsterdam's leading police department. A single long table and countless plain chairs were at its center, but its periphery was empty.

"Glad to see you both again," the chief said. "And Paul, one of our undercover informants tells me you're doing more police work than usual." He didn't ask them to be seated.

"I guess you'd say I get yanked into many investigations, but they and treasure hunting just naturally blend. Anyway, thanks for seeing us. I wish this were just a social call, but it's about the murders over here. And elsewhere."

"But before we go on," Otto said, "I just want you to know that I still don't have an office per se. Could have, but I'd rather be on the move around these four floors so I just use everyone else's if I have to look up something or copy something or do anything else that's done in an office. In other words, I feel freer the way it is."

Otto Bleeker was the shortest police executive Paul had ever come across. Standing a mere five-five, he made every effort to appear taller—erect, shoulders back, head held high. Almost fully bald, he was handsome to a degree, despite an irregular scar sweeping across his left cheek. Yet a broad and contagious smile all but obliterated the scar. He wore a wrinkled blue shirt, sleeves rolled up to his elbows, no tie, darker blue trousers with a thin belt that carried no gun or any other police paraphernalia. The way he was dressed and the layout of his office told Paul that Otto would rather roam the premises than be bogged down in a single location.

Paul summarized his responsibilities, stressing the six murders more than the stolen Blue Baron. "And, as you know, two of the victims were Danish. Plus they were members of *Gens de Vérité*. You remember that group, don't you?"

"Yes, but before continuing, the man you've got to speak to is Officer George Webley. He's new here but heads up that investigation. Came highly recommended from Great Britain. He's one flight down. I'll phone ahead and tell him to level with you, or, better still, I'll come along. Since the two murders here plus the four similar ones elsewhere—and I've *got* to say similar ... ghastly similar ... any of the officers you might run into on the way down might want to question you—even pat you down. Incidentally, are you still armed with those old-fashioned guns of yours?"

"Yes, sir, same ones.Ten years isn't too old."

It had finally become customary for Paul to start at the top—no matter the country—having learned the hard way that failing to do so was counterproductive and objectionable to the chain of command. Early on in his career, he would consult directly with a subordinate police officer and end up with scant information. His best friend, private investigator Dr. David Brooks and his wife Kathy, a police officer herself, had cautioned him about proper protocol, regardless of the size of a police jurisdiction or the country in which it was located. Yet it took him two years to begin complying. It wasn't such advice that tipped the scales; rather he'd grown tired of people claiming they'd deliver promises but never intending to in the first place because proper protocol hadn't been followed. Those in less authority would never admit to such unwritten "rules" for fear of some kind of vague reprisal. In any event, Paul had gone through Otto Bleeker this time around.

Webley's office was almost as vacant as Otto's, but it did have some bookcases, a computer, printer and copying machine. Young and rugged-looking, his height made up for the shortness of his boss. In contrast to Otto's attire, his white shirt was finely pressed, his military gray trousers were neatly creased, and strapped to his sides were a gun, a phone, handcuffs and a small flashlight. Paul was drawn mostly to the silver tagged cords wrapped loosely across his chest.

Because of the many windows and shards of light shining through, it would have otherwise been described as a dreary setting, but compared to Otto's quarters, Paul was impressed—though mildly.

Introductions completed, Webley explained, "We've tried to piece together the forensics of all six cases and what did we find so far? That the same gun was used. But there are a few leads to follow up on and perhaps you can do so—if you're willing."

"Willing?" Paul said emphatically. "I don't know where to begin, but I'm definitely willing."

"Well, as you know, whilst major crimes keep lingering in the public eye, the police get all sorts of calls and emails offering tips and suggestions. Most of the things that come in here are worthless, but amongst them, a few need looking into. Maybe three or four."

Paul thinned his lips. "Whilst?" he questioned. "Amongst?"

"Oh, sorry. That's part of the jargon from where I grew up in England. 'Whilst', not 'while', or 'amongst', not 'among'."

"Good. Amongst my thinking, that's how we'll start," Paul said, staring at Webley and smiling. Webley didn't return the smile.

"But what else?" Paul asked. He felt that the question was snappier than he'd intended and even that mimicking Webley was a mistake. Yet he followed with, "I mean, can you share with us anything else? Otto here called the murders 'ghastly'. How so?"

"Each victim was shot repeatedly—eight or ten times—as if the killer got a thrill out of each shot. A tiny diamond was found inserted into some of the wounds, both entry and exit. That's why we figured they were all killed by the same person. And I think he *wanted* the police to come to that conclusion."

"I see," Paul said, wishing he had brought along some crackers. "And those tiny diamonds ... worth anything?"

"I doubt it but ..."

Before he had a chance to elaborate, Otto intervened. "As I said over the phone, Paul, I've begun the usual police procedural. It's upstairs and I'll go get it. The informant who told me you're doing more police work also mentioned your interest in Napoleon Bonaparte, so I included him in the procedural."

Vincent had been listening to the interchange without comment, but now said, "No. I feel like an empty suit here, so I'll go up for it. You three continue on."

He rose and as he approached the doorway, Otto said, "It's on my desk in the green folder."

Officer Webley resumed his description of the tiny diamonds when, without warning, two shots rang out.

"The backstairs!" Otto shouted. "The backstairs!"

He and the other two raced to the exit door from Otto's office. Paul and the officer had drawn their guns. Before they had a chance to open the door, Vincent came through saying, "Bastard got away! He shot and missed and I shot and missed."

"You okay?" Paul asked, walking over and putting his arms around his shoulders.

"Yes, okay."

"Where do the stairs lead to?" Paul asked Otto.

"Just a back alley. No use going there. Probably had a car parked down below."

"And people can come and go through that back exit door?"

"There are doors like that on all four levels. After five o'clock, we lock them, but they're left unlocked from eight in the morning till then."

"Why not keep them locked all day?"

"Because some years ago, we had a group of wise guys barge into our offices with an intent to do harm. Word got around fast, but no one could come to our rescue through those doors."

Paul then inquired of Vincent, "So what happened up here?"

"Well, soon as I walked in, the exit door opened wide enough for me to see a gun sticking through … and part of a man's face. His shot missed me by a mile. I then shot back and didn't get him either. But guess what, Paul?"

"What?"

"His gun was tiny and pearl-handled. And I think he's got a mustache."

Paul's face grew chalky. "Volterraio Castle?" he asked.

"Could be."

"Christ, either tiny pearl-handled guns are popular or he's one of those goons from Elba."

Chapter 4

The two police officials and Vincent sat down uncomfortably, no doubt deep in thought, while Paul walked off to a corner of the office, smartphone in hand.

"Hi, Syl. First off, don't worry—we're alright. But things got pretty hairy here in Amsterdam's central police building." He described the past 15 minutes—which might have been 10 were it not for Sylvie's frequent questions.

"So I've made a definite decision and you come into play: please have those Connecticut security guards recommend a couple of them from Falmouth. Then hire them—for round-the-clock duty. Forget what they might charge, okay? And do you still have the gun in your handbag?"

"Yes. Will I need it?"

"I just don't know. After the surprise here, I have a funny feeling and I want both of us to be ready for anything."

"Are you coming home or continuing on? An organization called to ask if you'd lecture to them. The guy they'd invited took sick and canceled out. I know your lectures relax you. I don't know why, but they do. I told him you were out of the country."

"We're continuing on, but I might change my mind. I'll let you know. Tell the organization we'll get back to them soon." Paul's demeanor changed. "By the way, what organization called?"

"*The Cape Cod Police League* in Hyannis. It's their annual dinner. Frankly, I'd rather you be there than on foreign soil." Worry showed in her thickened voice.

"Substituting again," Paul said.

"But why not though? Look at the number of times you and David substituted for each other."

"Hmm ... maybe we should form a 'D'Arneau—Brooks Foundation."

She cleared her voice before asking, "You're continuing on? Where's that?"

"Haven't the slightest yet, but I'll phone you every day or two. If there's one positive thing that came out of what just happened, it's that we're now more on the alert for anything. Anyway, don't worry and I'd better hang up. The other guys are too quiet and they're staring at me."

"No, wait. One last question. How did the shooter know you'd be there and when you'd be there?"

"Same answer: haven't the slightest."

Paul returned to the others and said, "Just spoke to my wife. She's worried stiff now, but what the hell, I wanted her to have the usual guards back covering our house."

"You don't waste time, do you?" George asked.

"Never have, never will. Drives her crazy sometimes."

Otto had the police procedural in hand and read the following aloud:

Some of the countries or territories that Napoleon conquered:

Switzerland
Netherlands
Belgium
France
Spain
Kingdom of Italy
Corsica
Luxembourg
Croatia
Low countries
Grand Duchy of Warsaw

He then handed the document to Paul, who silently read the names of the victims, their cities, countries, and occupations.

>Amsterdam, Netherlands—Frelinghuyens, Willem—Electrician
>Amsterdam, Netherlands—Mulder, Jules—Accountant
>Luanda, Angola—Hoek, Erik—Journalist
>Freetown, Sierra Leona—Weston, Brian—Owner of travel agency
>Brussels, Belgium—Conklin, Claus—Real estate agent
>Sarajevo, Bosnia-Herzegovina—Danir Ademovic—Liquor store owner

Paul took out a card and wrote down all but the countries Napoleon had conquered. He knew those by heart. He next looked up at Otto and George, back at the procedural, then back at Otto, who asked, "Can we make anything out of this?"

"At this point I'd say no," Paul said, "except that Bosnia-Herzegovina stands out."

"I agree and I can explain that based on some other things the informant told me. He's got a theory."

"But wait," Paul said. "Who *is* your informant?"

"All I know is that he's German, goes by the name 'Gunther', and has been very helpful for a number of years now. He also works for the Hague."

Paul steepled his fingers. *Hmm, I have historians; the local police and the Hague have Gunther.*

"Does he get paid?"

"Plenty, but Administration takes care of it."

"And speaking of pay, could any of those six men have afforded to buy the diamond?" Paul asked.

"I wouldn't think so, but who knows? Maybe the killer knew something we don't. Anyway, Gunther's theory goes like this: until recently, the killer wanted to create what he termed a 'long overdue' blood diamond business in the Balkans. You've heard of Slobodan Milosevic, right? 'The Butcher of the Balkans'."

"Who hasn't?"

"Well, the killer was from Bosnia but moved away, according to Gunther. He—the killer, not Gunther—became raving mad over two things. First, he owned the Blue Baron, which, for years, he wanted to use as a drawing card in growing his business, but it was stolen from him. And second, he developed a hatred of both the life of Milosevic, who from the beginning had *opposed* the killer's plans to use the diamond as a drawing card, and of the Hague because they didn't act fast enough to punish such a terrible person. As I'm sure you're aware, Milosevic was turned over to the U.N. War Crimes Tribunal at the Hague for his atrocities, was on trial for four long years and died of a heart attack before a verdict could be reached. The bastard would have been held accountable for over 200,000 deaths. So because of all this, the killer went on a rampage."

Otto was obviously breathless. So were the other three, but not as obviously.

"So what do you make of the theory?" Otto asked, pretending to blow his nose with a handkerchief, but really wiping his brow.

"Complicated but conceivable," Paul said. He thought it the diplomatic way to phrase it, but he had some doubts. "So you trust him?" he asked.

"I do. Understand, it's just a theory, but probably should be looked into. Seems to me if it pans out, it makes your job—and mine—a lot easier."

"I can see that."

But Paul still had doubts. *It's too pat.*

The chief took a pad from his pocket and wrote down a line of notes. "I know you'll check with your own informants," he said, "so do me a favor."

"What's that?

"Let me know if you find any discrepancies."

"You can count on it, Otto, but let's go one step further. Let's check with each other regularly. Okay?"

"Perfect."

"And with that, we'd better get going. I'm anxious to see Fritz Van Camp at his brewery."

"Good guy."

"And one of our histarians ... I mean informants."

Before leaving, Paul asked Otto and George at the doorway: "When the killer lived in Bosnia, what did Gunther say he did for a living?"

"He never said and I never inquired. Did you, George?"

"No. Never did."

On the taxi ride to the Amsterdam Brewery at about 4 p.m., Paul and Vincent spent the time differently. Vincent napped while Paul believed it was an opportunity to engage in one of his internal monologues, combining it with thoughts about the beer industry. If there was one beverage he didn't like, it was just that: beer. Not breweries, but beer. He had in fact been to several brewing companies in connection with previous cases and always wondered, as he headed for each of them, why many suspects or middle-men operated or worked in them. Why were they drawn to such an environment? Once assured the tanks and kettles were clean and a measured degree of automation was reached for the day and the machinery was rolling, what more was there to do? Must be the same with soda manufacturing, right? Yes, but beer has greater clout than a bottle of Pepsi. Whether you're drinking it or selling it.

The brewery building up ahead could easily have passed for a compact oil refinery. Three large vertical tanks were pressed against a main structure on top, which was a variegated maze of steel fencing. They were let off near the front entrance and, after Paul had paid and dismissed the taxi driver, they marched directly toward Fritz Van Camp's office. It was definitely a march—Vincent even commented on it—for Paul was eager to get the historian's take on several issues, as he had done there before.

He and Fritz had exchanged key information regarding many past problems, both crime and gun related. Fritz had a firearms collection in his home's basement. Paul had visited it three times, finding it not unlike the one he had in his own basement. When traveling to the States, Fritz had always paid Paul a visit and never failed asking to see the collection. They would then have a good-natured tit for tat about whose was more impressive.

At the right side of the building, Paul and Vincent navigated a hallway—more like a tunnel—with overhead mirrors near every doorway. Paul could hear the mashing, filtering, fermenting and other processing steps emanating from their left side. Once at the doorway marked

"BREWMASTER", Fritz greeted them warmly and ushered them into his cluttered, non-descript office. All furniture there was made of metal—desk, chairs and tables.

Stocky, well over six-feet tall, face taut in anticipation, the histarian seemed to blend in with the surroundings and the business itself. His attire also appeared appropriate: sweat shirt, wraparound apron and a baseball cap with the lettering, "Chicago White Sox". He had purchased it while attending the Siebel Institute of Technology in the Lincoln Park neighborhood of that city. He'd chosen the Institute because it was the oldest brewing school in the United States and one of the oldest in the world. It was there that he had become acquainted with Paul, the two having collaborated in identifying a would-be arsonist who had flunked out of the school.

"Good to see you both once again," Fritz said. "Care for a beer?"

Each refused and the three sat in a grouping of chairs that Paul recognized as laser cut into powder-coated steel. The histarian reached over to his desktop for a blank card prior to the next question for Paul: "So you've gotten yourself involved again, eh?"

"Yeah. Usually I'm unsure of cases I've taken on. More so this one. I'll just plow along though and we'll see what happens. For starters over here, I just met with Otto Bleeker and his new associate, George Webley."

"Bleeker I know. Webley I don't."

"But as I told you in my call, I've got a number of things to check out, and that's where you come in, Fritz—along with the other histarians you've consulted with before. I'm just hoping you and those in your immediate area and in, of all places—the Balkans—can verify some things. Or, on the other hand, refute them."

"Got my card and pen. Go right ahead. And by the way, why do all histarians resort to a card instead of a piece of paper?"

Paul's response was immediate as if he'd expected the question. "Have you ever heard of a crumpled up card?"

"But why do all histarians work it that way?"

"I would suppose that, way back, two of them exchanged the same questions that we just did; they spoke about it to another pair who spoke about it to another, and so on. Then before long, pretty much all of us did the same thing. Used cards. In a way, it codifies us as a group."

"So we're a card-carrying group."

"Well put," Paul said.

He then presented the theory of Otto's informant, Gunther, stressing Bosnia, the stolen Blue Baron, Milosevic, The Hague and the killing rampage. Next, he produced his card containing the information about the six murder victims and, after waving it in the air with a smile and a flourish, read from it slowly so that Fritz could write it all down on his own card. Once that was over, Paul spoke about blood diamonds; about whether or not he should visit countries like Belgium, Sierra Leone, Bosnia-Herzegovina; and about the necessity of examining a picture that hung near Napoleon's sarcophagus.

"Any thoughts?" he asked.

"Off hand, you should definitely visit The Hague—maybe get some inside information about Milosevic and so on. It's only 30 miles from here. After that, will you be returning here, or near here?"

"Near here. Same hotel as always: Park Plaza Victoria. Even if they're booked, they always find a way to accommodate me."

"Good. I can lend you a car then. Leave it at the hotel when you return. Give the key to a front desk clerk. They all know me there. As for the other things—especially whether you should visit those countries—I'll check with the histarians I usually work with and get back to you as soon as possible. Again off hand, you'd be smart to look in on Belgium and Sierra Leona, at least. If you haven't heard from me by tomorrow, start with them. I mean after The Hague. And you know what draws my attention the most?"

"What?"

"The killer once living in Bosnia, and the fact that one of the victims was living and working there too."

Chapter 5

Up ahead, the imposing International Criminal Court Building in The Hague could be seen as six connected structures with a garden motif. The tallest had a green facade, was placed in the center of the design and was named the "Court Tower". It contained three courtrooms.

Paul parked near the Court Tower. He and Vincent entered it and headed in the direction of one of the courtrooms. By chance, they arrived in time to hear Knute Larsen, from the Office of the Prosecutor, introduce himself to a legion of tourists. They stood quietly toward the rear and listened in as he began a talk.

Thank you all for being here. I know you must have signed the poster in the corridor indicating I'd be talking about

Baltic history and about Slobodan
Milosevic, the so-called 'Butcher of the
Balkans'. He and the days involving the
republics and provinces in that region are
almost inconceivable.

He then spent a half-hour giving particulars
about Slovenia, Bosnia-Herzgovina, Montenegro,
Macedonia and Serbia, including the autonomous
province called Kosovo. He spoke of The Hague,
so-called "ethnic cleansing", the Balkan's history
during both World Wars, and NATO's bombing of
military targets throughout the Yugoslavia area.

Then, nearly another half-hour on the
establishment of an Independent State of Croatia by
the Axis powers of Germany, Italy, Hungary and
Bulgaria. These countries, he said, became a Nazi
puppet state that soon created concentration camps
for anti-fascists, communists, Serbs, Jews and
gypsies. "So-called Chetniks arose and they
became allies of the United States in Europe and
the communist Yugoslav National Liberation
Army, led by Josip Tito. At first, the Chetniks were
successful in widespread guerrilla warfare, but the
Germans countered, the results totaling 1.7 million
casualties."

But his main focus was on Milosevic, a
dictator who, he said, orchestrated atrocities
beyond belief—atrocities that resulted in the deaths
and/or brutalization of millions of people. Forced
deportation of women, children and old men was

highlighted, as were the burned bodies and mass graves of fighting-age men. "During a decade of violence and terror," Larson continued, "many felt that the dictator's basic motivation amounted to a search for power. Power that was augmented by condoning the use of trucks containing bodies either packed upright or lying horizontally."

Paul cringed and, with eyes that became pinpoints of fire, he fought off an urge to rise up and demand that the Prosecutor discontinue the talk, and to complain: "My head is reeling: such splitting of territories, such savagery ... hard to conceive of it all."

The prosecutor ended with three conclusions that were delivered nearly an octave higher than before. One, Milosevic was eventually turned over to the United Nations War Crimes Tribunal at The Hague and charged with crimes against humanity in Kosovo and Croatia, and with genocide in general. Two, that he had become the first head of state to face an international war crimes court. And three, that his four-year trial had not been completed because he died of a heart attack.

Both Paul and Vincent found a bench to sit on and finished off taking notes.

"I wish there had been more on ethnic cleansing," Paul said. "I'm beginning to put together my own theory ... but it needs some tweaking. Let's shove off. Disturbing but valuable. Not sure in what way, but definitely valuable."

Back in the car, he looked over his notes and added a few more. Vincent did the same. "Maybe we can compare once at the hotel," he said. Paul nodded and, as he inserted the ignition key, he added, "And that's enough for The Hague. This confirms what Gunther said about Milosevic and it gives us more to go on."

"More? How so?"

"Remember what he said about the killer's Blue Baron being stolen after his wanting to use it as a drawing card to grow a diamond business? Well, let's just file that away for now. I've got to give it more thought."

Vincent didn't press him further.

Paul started the car while entertaining a question more than a decision: "Diamond Cleansing?"

In less than half an hour, he parked the car at a side lot of the Park Plaza Victoria. Vincent walked briskly into the hotel but Paul ambled in, and after handing the key to a desk clerk with the directive of what Fritz had provided him, he and Vincent registered for the same room. There, Vincent began to bombard him with questions, but Paul begged off, stating he just wanted to sit and think something through.

"I've got an important decision to make," he said.

He knew it was time for another internal monologue but, for once, he asked himself why he called it that. He preferred to label it a "stream of consciousness", and he wouldn't hesitate to explain to anyone that he doesn't talk to himself; rather he becomes conscious of a steady mix of thoughts that need straightening out. In this instance, the paramount thought was whether or not to continue on to Belgium, Sierra Leone and Angola or to give in to a compelling desire to postpone such a schedule for a brief period. Possibly to lecture, for as only he and Sylvie understood, it was a strong way to relax—although unusual.

But a trip home isn't just to satisfy the idea of lecturing; it's the relief from strain, and a day or two of rest.

He was convinced he needed it in full measure especially after hearing the details of Milosevic's savagery. But even beyond that, the encounters with Otto, with George, and with Fritz—plus the sudden exchange of gunfire involving Vincent—and all on the same day— weighed heavily on his mind. He couldn't recall the last time an assortment of issues had hit him as hard. It wasn't the number of encounters that were faced; it was the emotion they triggered: pointed, profound, draining. He was most comfortable when dealing with others and their concerns, not when wrapped up in himself, as he was now. His forehead moist, his heart scrambling, neck muscles tingling—it was all a recognizable warning to shift his attention, to curtail plans to continue on, in favor of returning home for a spell.

If I had known what was in store for us, I would have planned on two separate trips in the first place. That might have helped.

He looked out a window. The moon, though full, appeared more distant than usual, yet lit up the sky enough to contrast with Paul's dark mood.

He seemed to snap out of the stream of consciousness when he faced Vincent and said, "Let's go back to the States for a few days. How about it?"

Vincent folded his arms on his chest before responding. "I knew you were thinking of that, and I don't blame you. It's been an intense trip. Will do us both good."

"I'll notify Fritz and Leon first, then Sylvie so she's not shocked when I arrive home. I don't think I have to call Otto or George, though."

The first two calls were mirror images of one another: "I have some important things to tend to at home—might take a few days," Paul said. "But then it's on to Angola, Sierra Leona and Belgium, because interviewing the victims' families is absolutely necessary." He didn't figure he was fibbing regarding the visit home, because some rest and a possible lecture qualified as "important things" in his mind. Both Fritz and Leon expressed an understanding, with the former adding that he hadn't yet completed his contacts with histarians.

Finally, the call to his Syl. It was about 2 p.m. in the U.S. "It's me again."

"You still alright?"

"Yeah, but I'm returning home. Should be there around one a.m." He knew that in just a few words, he was coming across as unhinged, yet asked, "And about that lecture request: is it scheduled soon, by any chance?"

"I can't believe the timing! Captain Burns from the Police League called again. Their dinner is tomorrow night and they still don't have a speaker. He was wondering if you were back yet."

Paul could feel a toothy grin blossoming on his face. "Fantastic! Do call back and say I'd be happy to fill in. I'll bring you up to date when I get home. We accomplished a lot, but it wore us out. Plan on my sleeping and sleeping."

"You better. And what should I tell Burns you'll talk about."

"Oh … ah … let's see. I'm thinking of the JonBenet Ramsey case. Haven't done that one in a long time. It'll show how **not** to investigate a case."

Chapter 6

Bright and early the next morning—Friday—they left for the States. Their roles were reversed this time: Vincent appeared deep in thought while Paul napped for most of the way.

On landing at the Joint Base Cape Cod airport, they agreed to settle on the time of their return flight to the Balkans. "I'll phone you early next week," Paul said. "You can still afford the time off?"

"I'd *make* it affordable. You rest up now."

"You, too, although you don't look as worn out as I feel."

"That's because you have a stronger vested interest in the whole mess."

Paul's last words before they split up were, "And a mess it is."

A drenching summer air smelled damp and clean when Paul arrived home. But the raindrops that pelted his face as he scurried from limo to front door did little to ease his exhaustion. He came across no security guards and reasoned they just hadn't been hired yet.

Once again, Sylvie had waited up for him, meeting him at the doorway. Her eyes were moist, his dry and half-closed. They remained speechless as they embraced for a longer time than usual. Finally Paul insisted she retire for the night.

"I'll join you after I unwind for a few minutes, provided I don't fall asleep standing up."

"No, I can wait, Paul. Just force yourself to tell me what you accomplished over … over … there."

"Plenty," he said, "but too much for one guy—make that two—in such a short time."

"Why didn't you spread it out?"

"I intended to but one thing just naturally led to another."

"Oh," she said, "before I forget. I wasn't able to reach Captain Burns."

"No problem. I'll handle it."

She was wearing a see-through nightgown, and after excusing himself to visit the bathroom for a quick shower, he came out nude, picked her up and carried her toward their bed. He set her down gently, mildly aware that she expected some intimacy. Instead, he crawled in next to her, pulled the covers up and folded his hands behind his head. Somewhat more alive, he summarized what had transpired overseas, focusing on the "overwhelming" lecture at The Hague. He indicated it was the turning point in the decision to return home.

"But just for a brief period. There's still so much to do. In the Balkan cities. In whatever other cities that leads us to. In Paris. We'll take the Thalys Bullet. And by the way, Vincent will be with me ... he'll be ... with me. Did I say Paris? That's where we check on the picture ... on the painting. Something wrong there."

Paul was beginning to sound disjointed but before falling off to sleep, he said he'd contact old friend Burns later that morning to indicate that if they still had no speaker for their dinner, he would gladly be that person.

It was not unusual for him to spend a fitful night, tossing between wakefulness and whisking dreams, but not this time. He awoke at 11 a.m. The only thing on his mind was to contact the captain and offer his services. He nearly lost his balance as he rolled out of bed, looked up the Hyannis Police Department's phone number in a nearby directory, dialed it and learned that the League was still without a speaker for the dinner. He agreed to pitch in. He saw that Sylvie had left for work—no doubt a couple of hours late—so he plopped back into bed.

From the time of his mid-afternoon reawakening to Sylvie's return from the Oceanographic Institute, Paul did little that was constructive around the house. He mostly read up on the history of countries he would soon visit: Angola, Belgium and Sierra Leone. *Or should it be Bosnia first?* His investigative work had taken him to all four countries in the past, but he had never read about their histories. Not that it would have made any difference this time around, he thought, but it had at least given him something to do besides walking around and thinking of the JonBenet Ramsey case.

When Sylvie returned home, she was too tired even to talk much, and especially to prepare a dinner. And since Paul didn't care to throw together one of his tasteless meals, he left for their favorite "take out" restaurant and reappeared to find her back in bed. He let her sleep away and joined her at about six, never recalling what he had eaten.

The next day dragged on, and about an hour before he left for the speaking engagement, he grew more spirited. Perhaps Sylvie's earlier comment had helped : "You've looked as unproductive as a slinking turtle."

During the entire 20-minute drive from Falmouth to Hyannis, Paul noticed the same black car in his rearview mirror. When he slowed down, it slowed down; when he sped up, it sped up. He entered a back parking lot at the Cape Codder

Resort and Spa and so did the black car. It passed him and pulled into a space three cars away.

Paul withdrew the Stealth 9 mm from his ankle rig and placed it on his lap. It was only until he briefly observed a male driver and a female passenger emerging from the black car that he relaxed and replaced the gun.

Inside, a side conference room was standing-room-only for 300 or so attendees. Paul recognized many officers who came from Hyannis and surrounding towns on the Cape, and he waved to them all. Captain Burns appeared out of nowhere and after a prolonged handshake, ushered him to a seat at the head table. The ensuing meal, small talk and introduction of police dignitaries were overshadowed by Paul's frequent glances at a couple seated directly in front of him, not 25 feet away. *Where have I seen them? The black car!*

Captain Burns' introduction of Paul was short, to the point, and included alluding to the fact that he had "come to our rescue as a speaker." The applause was prolonged and deafening as Paul gulped down some remaining drops of water before he rose and headed for the podium, folder in hand. He began with thanks to the Captain, with appreciation for the opportunity to speak to many old friends, and then continued:

I'd like to talk about JonBenet Ramsey. It'll become obvious that physical evidence was terribly ruined in this case. And I must explain: a good deal of what I say about it will come from notes before me which, in turn, came from a book that famous forensic scientist, Dr. Henry Lee, and I coauthored.

He could feel himself already unwinding, his hands steadier, his smile coming more easily. Even eye contact with the black car couple became friendlier.

So ... as murder cases go, Sacco-Vanzetti had its nearly six years of appeals, JFK had its years of mishandling evidence, and Sam Sheppard had its years of wrongful incarceration. What about JonBenet? Was it a perfect crime? Or was its solution bogged down by crime scene issues and/or law enforcement infighting? I present this to you not only because it has spellbound people everywhere, but also because it's a prototypical example of how **not** to handle a criminal investigation, especially the all-important crime scene. Many authorities claim the case was fraught with forensic errors from the outset.

The story begins with a frantic 911 call received by the Boulder, Colorado Police Department at 5:52, the morning after

Christmas 1996. The caller was Patsy Ramsey who shrieked that her six-year-old daughter had been abducted from their home during the night. Patsy and her husband, John, were members of Boulder's socially elite. Their home was a sprawling Tudor-style structure. Their son, Burke, was said to be asleep upstairs. Two other children from John's first marriage were away from home at the time: John Andrew Ramsey, 20, a University of Colorado student was visiting in Atlanta; while Melinda Ramsey Long, 25, a nurse, lived in Atlanta with her husband, a medical doctor.

Patsy had been grooming her daughter because of her own failure to be crowned Miss America as a Miss West Virginia entry. Listen to some of JonBenet's beauty contest awards:

—America's Royal Miss
—Colorado State All-Star Kids Cover Girl
—Little Miss Michigan
—Little Miss Colorado
—Little Miss Merry Christmas
—Little Miss Sunburst
—National Tiny Miss Beauty.

Sad! I get choked up even thinking about it. Anyway, police arrived at 6:10 a.m.

and from that point forward, the case dragged on for years as a stormy mixture of tragedy, investigative ineptness, controversy, accusations of payoffs and alleged cover-ups.

The parents informed the police that Patsy had descended the stairway from their third floor bedroom to make coffee, and on the bottom step, she reportedly found a three-page note. It's rather long and definitely chilling but I must read it to you:

Mr. Ramsey,

Listen carefully! We are a group of individuals that represent a small foreign faction. We respect your business but not the country that it serves. At this time we have your daughter in our possession. She is safe and unharmed and if you want her to see 1997, you must follow our instructions to the letter.

You will withdraw $118,000.00 from your account. $100,000 will be in $100 bills and the remaining $18,000 in $20 bills. Make sure you bring an adequate size attache to the bank. When you get home you will put the money in a brown paper bag. I will call you between 8 and 10 a.m. tomorrow to instruct you on delivery. The delivery will be exhausting so I advise you to be rested. If we monitor you getting the money early, we might call you early to arrange an earlier delivery of the money and hence an earlier pick-up of your daughter.

Any deviation of my instructions will result in the immediate execution of your daughter. You will also be denied her remains for proper burial. The two gentlemen watching over your daughter do not particularly like you so I advise you not to provoke them. Speaking to anyone about your situation, such as the police, F.B.I., etc, will result in your daughter being beheaded. If we catch you talking to a stray dog, she dies. If you alert bank authorities, she dies. If the money is in any way tampered with, she dies. You will be scanned for electronic devices and if any are found, she dies. You can try to deceive us but be warned that we are familiar with law enforcement countermeasures and tactics. You stand a 99% chance of killing your daughter if you try to outsmart us. Follow our instructions and you stand a 100% chance of getting her back. You and your family are under constant scrutiny as well as the authorities. Don't try to grow a brain, John. You are not the only fat cat around so don't think that killing will be difficult. Don't underestimate us, John. Use that good southern common sense of yours. It's up to you now, John!

Victory!

S.B.T.C.

Paul scanned the room and observed every police officer leaning forward. Some were rubbing their bottom lip. Others had disbelief plastered over their faces. And it looked as though all had stopped eating dessert, spoons straight up in their sundaes. It was as if they didn't want to make a sound.

I suppose I'd better comment on that "S.B.T.C." I'm told it stands for, "Shall Be The Conqueror". How it applies here? I don't know. But what I do know is that there are three unusual things about the note that I'd like to call to your attention. One is the use of the word "small" at the very beginning. Foreign factions or terrorist groups don't typically call themselves "small". Two is the amount of money asked for. It's exactly what John Ramsey's bonus was: $118,000. And three is the word, "hence". Most people would use the word, "so" or "therefore". Now I'm not insinuating anything, but in the examination of many of Patsy's old letters, she frequently used the word, "hence". I'd simply call this "coincidental".

Now, after police officers arrived, they conducted a search of the premises but failed to examine a small basement room. As we all know, the entire house was a crime scene and should have been secured, but they allowed Patsy and John to admit their pastor and some old friends. They then roamed around, in effect ruining any possible forensic evidence.

Once again, I'm not insinuating anything but I have to comment on some strange behavior. Patsy was described as sobbing but without tears; John was cool and collected. First officers on the scene stated they were struck by the peculiar way Patsy covered her eyes as if in tears, while furtively peering between her fingers to glace around the room. They also reported that there was no physical contact between the parents, who hardly spoke to nor made eye contact with one another.

Police reports indicated that photographs showed areas of melting snow in the immediate vicinity of the house, but there were no footprints near the basement window. A controversial addendum was that fully intact cobwebs stretched over the window. Nor was there any indication of forced entry. But there was a notation that the window was slightly broken, and that, inside, a blue suitcase was in place directly beneath it. John later explained that he'd broken the window during the summer when he accidentally locked himself out of the house.

By 10:30 a.m., something also most strange. No ransom call had been received, so what does John do? You'd think a distraught father would wait around indefinitely but, instead, he went downtown to pick up the family mail! Another question: Why would the police have allowed this to happen?

Then an hour after his return, John and two of his friends were asked to search the house again. He went to the basement and was soon heard screaming. He had discovered JonBenet's lifeless body in a small room that was considered a "wine cellar". She was wrapped in a white blanket, which he pulled away. He next ripped off some duct tape that covered her mouth. A garrote of white cord was embedded in her neck while another was wrapped loosely around her right wrist. The broken off handle of a wooden paint brush was so placed that it could have been used to tighten the cord around her neck. Some believed the crime was made to look like auto-erotic asphyxiation, but there was no evidence of sexual assault. No penetration, for example. A few marks in her genital area were attributed to the splits she did in her dance routines. Others remarked that scattered marks on other parts of JonBenet may have been due to the use of a stun gun. But most believed they were connected to a child's toy found near her body.

John carried her upstairs and placed her on the living room floor, thus creating another crime scene. He hovered over her, moaning without tears and, like his wife before, his eyes reportedly darted around the room to see if anyone was watching.

Let me read the final diagnoses in the autopsy report:

1. Ligature strangulation
   A. Circumferential ligature with associated ligature furrow of neck
   B. Abrasions and petechial hemorrhages, neck
   C. Petechial hemorrhages, conjunctival surfaces of eyes and skin of face
2. Craniocerebral injuries
   A. Scalp contusion
   B. Linear, comminuted fracture of right side of skull
   C. Linear pattern of contusions of right hemisphere

D. Subarachnoid and subdural hemorrhage

E. Small contusions, tips of temporal lobe

3. Abrasion of right cheek

4. Abrasion/contusion, posterior right shoulder

5. Abrasions of right lower back and posterior left lower leg

6. Abrasion and vascular congestion of vaginal mucosa

7. Ligature of right wrist

8. Dotted pattern injuries on cheek and body

Many questions have been raised concerning specific aspects of the crime. Some I've answered already but all bear repeating:

1. Was she sexually assaulted?

2. She died of strangulation and head trauma. Which came first?

3. Was it an inside job, or was there an intruder?

4. Was a stun gun used?

5. Why was the exact amount of John's yearly bonus—$118,000—used as the ransom demand?

6. Was the ransom note bogus? A common theme among analysts was that since there

was a ransom note left in the house, there shouldn't have been a murdered child in the basement. And, conversely, since a dead child was in the house, there shouldn't have been a ransom note on the stairs.

What followed were years of bickering by city officials, much media frenzy and a 13-month grand jury probe, which culminated in the district attorney's announcement that there was insufficient evidence to file charges against anyone. About five years ago, so-called "touch" DNA was extracted from the waistband of the long johns the child had been wearing, but it was decided that the DNA belonged to either medical or law enforcement personnel. And finally along these lines, it was announced, just a few days ago in fact, that prior to her death two years later—from ovarian cancer—Patsy revealed in an interview that she had a severe emotional breakdown requiring psychiatric care three years before her daughter's death. But that subsequently she had nothing to do with the murder.

At about the same time as that interview, a local resident named Michael Helgoth was cited as being one of two men who were responsible for the death. Helgoth himself was later found murdered. Complex, to say the least, but the best I can come up with is that probably the case may *never* be solved.

I'll wind things up here with two more things to read to you. One is a list of forensic specialists consulted, and the other is my feeling about double scenarios for the case. First then, the list. I hope its length doesn't bore you, but I've got to say that the number who took part is the largest I've ever known about, either here or abroad.

DNA experts
Sexual abuse and assault experts
Child abuse consultants
Specialists in violent crime
Forensic pathologists
Psychological profilers
Juvenile witness interview specialists
Advocates for incest survivors
Consultant for chemical breakdown of
     trace evidence
Linguistic experts
Forensic knot specialist
Stun gun expert
Fingerprint experts
Expert in terrorism (ransom note study)
Crime scene reconstruction experts
Handwriting experts (ransom note)
Fiber experts

Ink, paper experts
Spider expert
Plant experts
Legal consultants
Medical experts

But despite such a dazzling array of experts, there has been no closure in Boulder.

Then the two scenarios:

A. Supporting an intruder theory:
     1. Broken basement window and scuff marks on the inside surface of the wall.
     2. Dotted injury patterns on her body resembling patterns possibly made by a stun gun.
     3. Small amount of foreign DNA found on her fingernails and on her underwear.
     4. Ransom note found in the house.
     5. The Ramseys passed a polygraph (lie detector) test.
     6. Signs of possible sexual assault.

B. Supporting an insider theory:
     1. Peculiar behavior of Patsy and John.

2. The place where body was found was clearly a secondary location within the primary scene.

3. The "wine cellar" in the basement is located in a back room. Layout of the house is such that only a person familiar with the house would be able to find that room.

4. Language used in the ransom note is unlike that found in the typical ransom note of a kidnapper.

5. The ink and paper used for the ransom message originated from the Ramsey house.

6. A partial note containing similar printing was found in a garbage can in the house. A practice note?

7. The amount of foreign DNA found on her fingernails and underpants was extremely minute. Contamination?

The talk had been relatively short but fulfilled both Paul's obligation and his desire to lecture. And except for the most recent Michael Helgoth portion, he had given the talk many times before. When it was over this time, however, he discovered that he had never received such an enthusiastic ovation. He was hoping the black car couple would be leading it. But they had left a few minutes earlier and Paul wondered why.

During it all, he could think of only two words: "mesmerized" as applied to the 300-person audience and "therapeutic" as applied to himself. The end came with his usual closing remark: "Thank you for having me here and for your attention."

Captain Burns approached Paul and congratulated him in glowing terms. "Maybe you could speak to us again sometime," he said. "Our big dinner is an annual one, but we could schedule another one at a moment's notice. Even in a week or two. How about it?"

Paul wasn't prepared for the question and simply said, "Thank you, but speak about what?"

Burns didn't hesitate: "Well, I happen to know you admire Napoleon and have written some books about him. I like him, too. Maybe *he* could be your subject."

Paul was taken by surprise and instead of a yes or no answer, decided to be noncommittal: "He was certainly controversial, wasn't he?"

"Maybe, but his good side outweighed his bad side."

"Good way of putting it. Look, Captain, I've got my hands full right now, traveling all over the place, but I'll think about it and get back to you. I must reassure you though—if there's a natural break in what I'm doing, I'll come back. Maybe you might inform your members of that and schedule a dinner, say two weeks from now? And another thing: if I don't choose Napoleon, perhaps another topic?"

"Any subject at all. It's up to you. You'd be well received."

Once in his car, he couldn't tell the difference between repeated sighs and shortness of breath. He forced himself to relax after finally concluding they were both related to the anxiety of a finished—and successful—lecture. Plus the captain's unexpected request. Paul was also anxious to return home where he knew Sylvie would be waiting for his comments.

She was not surprised at Paul's successful presentation. "See," she said, "no matter what, you impress."

"But this one could have gone either way."

"Oh, you always say that. Give yourself some credit for a change."

Paul beamed and gave her a military salute while saying, "Aye-aye, ma'am."

He then remembered to inform her of the black car couple leaving early. "I wonder why?" he said.

"Who knows? Maybe one of them had to hit the head."

"But maybe not."

They were both behind in their sleep and spent the next day, Sunday, resting and discussing almost everything irrelevant.

PART THREE

Chapter 7

Back in Amsterdam's Park Plaza Hotel on Monday, their usual airplane at the ready, Paul and Vincent were about to leave for their "tri-city" inquiry, starting with Luanda, Angola's capital city. Paul's smartphone vibrated and it was Fritz calling, as he said he would.

"Honestly, Paul, I received more information from my fellow histarians than I ever expected to. People, places, things—you name it. They all checked with others before giving me their advice. Seems like I've been on the phone twenty-four-seven. Anyway, I have it all written down … you ready for it?"

"Absolutely! I'm ready."

"Well, sorry if I start sounding like a teacher … an instructor or something … but it's the best way to give it all to you."

"I understand, Fritz. And I'm anxious to hear."

"First of all, go to Luanda, Angola; then to Freetown, Sierra Leone; and then to Brussels, Belgium. Naturally, you'll want to commiserate with the families of the victims, but also try to find out all you can about them—the victims, I mean. And I never pressed any of them on this, but they were unanimous in recommending your saving Sarajevo, Bosnia and Amsterdam here for last."

"Maybe they feel those will take the most time."

"Maybe. But they also said that you should even check on police officials at all locations."

"Police officials? Why's that?"

"Because they might have an inside track to sensitive information. The kind they never wanted to share with the media, for example."

"See, this is the sorta stuff I never would have thought of, Fritz." Paul's face had grown pensive.

"C'mon now, you just haven't been an historian as long as I have—or as long as my friends have."

"Good. Let's call it that way," Paul replied lamely.

"And the final piece of advice seems like it might yield a lot. They all brought up the names of others you might talk to and it's funny, you know: they were in agreement—solid agreement—as to who they were. This, I did press them on. The guys I'm about to mention, and I have it right here ... they each had a gripe with the victim in their city. I don't know the specifics of the gripes, but you should find out."

"Will do. There might be a common thread."

"Could be. Maybe something along those lines. So here they are—names, cities and languages they speak. Sorry, but I don't have their occupations:

Adao Candido; Luanda, Angola; Portuguese
Victor Breitenbach; Brussels, Belgium; Dutch
Adam James; Freetown, Sierra Leone; English.

Paul read back the list for Fritz's verification.

"So that should keep you busy, Paul. Good luck and let me know how things are going, okay?"

"I'll do that—but one final comment, and I hope you don't take this personally. I wish you came up with the name of the killer and where the Blue Baron is."

"Good point. In fact a key point. We discussed it and got nowhere. They agreed that something's blocking those issues, but they don't know what. Nor do I. This happens once in a while and I'm sorry, but if anything pops up, you'll be the first to hear about it."

"Okay, and many, many thanks."

He hung up, faced Vincent and, blowing out from puffed cheeks, said, "Christ, why did I take this on? I ask you … why?"

"Don't ask *me*. I'm just along for the ride."

"Thank God, or I'd go nuts. If I start acting strange, find me the nearest psychiatric ward."

Paul almost forgot, but then remembered to contact Otto at Police Headquarters.

Another phone call!

"We're here in Amsterdam again, Otto. Same hotel. This is obvious, but we never talked about it. Could you have the local police departments contact the families in Luanda and Freetown and Brussels? We can't just barge in on the victims' relatives. It would probably be best if you told the police to introduce us as Americans who work closely with police all over the world. You have a list of the cities. Do get the family's addresses and phone numbers and please call me when you have them. I'll notify the families regarding when we expect to arrive. How's that sound?"

Vincent nodded his approval.

"Sounds like the best way to handle it," Otto said. "I'll get right on it."

After hanging up, Paul sat down to think a couple of things through. They confused him some, but he couldn't determine why. First, the suggested order of visits—starting with the country that was farthest away … Angola … and working north to Sierra Leone, and north again, ending up in nearby Belgium. *Isn't it backwards? There must be a reason.* He was likewise confused by the suggestion that he save Bosnia and Amsterdam for last. *Why's that?*

Second, he guessed he'd be consulting with more police departments than any other departments in any other countries he'd visited in the past.

The flip side, however—more positive— was that he estimated the flight time to Luanda would be about eight hours (commercial flight time), but seven hours (JBCC flight time). Just enough of a respite to bring his sleep needs up to a healthy state—finally. But before leaving the plane, he did manage to read a brief summary of Luanda as presented in a folder he'd brought along in his satchel. It was a capsulized version of what he'd read about Angola two days before. That article, in itself, was an extraction and so he beamed while thinking of the following as an extraction of an extraction:

Luanda is the capital of Angola, and the country's most populous and important city and primary port. It is located on

Angola's coast on the Atlantic Ocean and is both the country's main seaport and administrative center. It has a population of over six million and is the world's third most populous Portuguese-speaking city, behind only Brazil's Sao Paulo and Rio de Janeiro. Luanda is divided into two parts: the Baixa de Luanda (lower Luanda, or the old city) and the Cidade Alta (upper Luanda, or the new city).The Baixa de Luanda is situated next to the port. Narrow and deserted walkways wind their way along water's edge and on the opposite side are scattered stores and florist shops.

The Dondo Railway Station is the most convenient way to explore Angola from its capital while white and blue taxis called Candongueiros are everywhere to be found. There are endless lines of them at all airports.

The city is home to most of Angola's educational institutions, including the public University of Agostinho and the private Catholic University of Angola. It is also the location of a massive stadium that seats over 60,000.

They had departed Amsterdam at nine a.m. and arrived at the Angola International Airport at around 3:15 p.m. No sooner had the plane touched down than Paul felt his smartphone vibrate again.

Otto was calling with the information Paul wanted about the three families they'd be visiting. He wrote all of it down in his pad, thanked the chief, and assured him he'd call him after the first visit.

"Who did you speak to?" he asked.

"The wife."

"And how did it go?"

"Fairly well. Apparently she and her two teen-agers are handling the loss as best they can. Their church has helped out a lot."

"What did she say about my going there?"

"She's looking forward to it."

"I think I'll call her right now then and get directions. Does she live in a house or an apartment?

"A high-rise apartment. And forgive me for interceding but you might skip getting directions because I assume you'll be taking a taxi. Just giving the driver the address might be enough."

Paul and Vincent found a bench to sit on and Paul dialed Mrs. Erik Hoek's phone number. "Mrs. Hoek?"

"Yes?"

"This is Paul D'Arneau calling. My associate and I are at the airport and we were wondering if this is a good time for us to come over."

"Yes, the police chief told me it would be soon."

"Good. Are you nearby?"

"Not too far. You have a car or will you take a taxi?"

"A taxi. Looks like they're all over the place."

"Well, the drivers are very good. I understand you have our location—it's the first high-rise after the stadium. He can drop you off there ... we're on the fifth floor ... or you can come from the other direction."

"The other direction?"

"Yes, it's a shorter way, a prettier way. And you avoid all the traffic. The only problem is that you have to walk along a dirt road ... not too far though."

They were left off at the start of a crushed stone walkway and began walking past the types of stores that Paul had read about. The only one that seemed open for business, though, was a florist shop. Fifty yards beyond that, Vincent stopped short and said, "Got an idea, Paul. Why don't I go back to the florist place and buy some flowers for Mrs. Hoek?"

"Fine idea. Always thinking. Always thinking. I'll wait here."

Vincent headed back and as soon as he entered the shop, two men with menacing smiles approached Paul, one from each side. To him they looked a foot taller and broader than he was. There was no time to withdraw the Stealth 9 mm from his ankle rig because the men leaped forward and grabbed him by the shoulders. But he *did* have time to execute what had taken four years to master at Bruno's Martial Arts Studio, and was known as the BKM or bilateral karate maneuver. It was a karate chop using both hands simultaneously against two opponent's arms and, at the same time, launching a leg sweep at each of them. Paul executed the maneuver with swiftness and dexterity and, in the process, fell to the ground and arose without injury. Meanwhile, the men plummeted down heavily, groaned for a full 60 seconds, then managed to scramble to their feet and disappear into a cluster of trees. No words were exchanged and Paul gave them a ceremonial bow as they left.

He was elated that he had had full command of the situation but couldn't help wondering how the attackers knew of his destination and precisely when he'd arrive there. *Or was I a mistake? Did they pick on the wrong guy?*

The elation was combined with appreciation directed at his close friend, Dr. David Brooks, for convincing him to join Bruno's as an eventual instructor in tae kwan do and atemiwaza. Through devoted study and performance, Paul first earned a black belt in half the usual time—two years. He was then given the responsibility of teaching judo students—or "judoka"—how to fall safely and how to strengthen the muscles used in judo. After learning to fall in all directions and from all positions without injuring themselves, he helped them acquire skills involving a foot sweep, hip throw, rear throw, shoulder throw, and various hand chops. In addition, he emphasized the importance of judo etiquette, including ceremonial bows, like the one he had just given. And on further consideration, he felt that being the wrong person attacked was unlikely. But if so, he was still left with why, where and when. *Why me, what location and what time?*

Shortly thereafter, Paul saw Vincent returning from the flower shop and decided not to mention the encounter for fear it might dampen what lay ahead. Vincent was carrying a narrow box with a cellophane top. He tipped it toward Paul who commented favorably on the long-stemmed, multicolored roses that shown through: reds, pinks, yellows and whites.

The apartment's living room was what Paul often called "over-furnished" and its pleasing aroma indicated it had recently been sprayed with an air sanitizer. As Mrs. Hoek ushered the two men into the room, she said, "Come in … do come in." Bare-legged, she wore a dark dress and dark shoes. Black bobbed hair was cut straight around her head at jaw level and included a fringe at the front.

"Thank you for having us, Mrs. Hoek," Paul said.

"No. Call me Freda."

"Alright … Freda. I'm Paul and this is Vincent, my assistant."

They shook hands and Vincent handed her the flowers.

"How kind of you," she said, "but you didn't have to."

They sat in three chairs that had been pulled together at the far end of the room.

Paul wasn't sure if it was the right way to begin when he asked, "You have two sons, they told me."

"Yes, but they're at a school function."

"Oh, we would have liked to meet them. But how are *you* doing?"

"Fairly well for a 40-year-old widow." Her taut face was that of a woman fifteen-years older.

Paul decided it best to get to the matters they were there for. "We won't take up too much of your time, Freda, so may I ask you some questions and if you don't care to answer, just say so?"

"Yes, that's fine."

"And you wouldn't mind if Vincent here took down some notes?"

"No, not at all."

"Do you know Adao Candido?"

"Yes. He's a lawyer who claimed my husband cheated him out of a fee."

"A fee for what?"

"I don't know."

"Your husband—Erik is it?"

"Yes ... Erik."

"He was a journalist?"

"Yes."

"Could the claim have anything to do with articles he wrote?"

"I don't know about that, either."

Paul looked at Vincent who, it appeared, was writing things on a pad word-for-word. Paul took out his own pad, skimmed over topics he'd previously scribbled on it, sized up his options, then checked his watch. All within seconds.

Vincent seemed to be relieved as he flexed his writing hand. Freda's face turned vacant.

"Now about that famous diamond …" Paul continued.

"The Blue Baron." It was a statement, not Freda's own question.

"The expensive Blue Baron. Was your husband planning on buying it?"

"Not 'buying it', but he was just 'interested' in it, and he told everybody he was. We could never have afforded it."

Paul ran his hand over his mouth as if to cover a grin of satisfaction.

"I understand," he said. "Now you're probably aware of this, but the two elements that authorities feel were the motives for Erik's and five other murders are their speaking publicly about, one, buying the diamond and, two, speaking about Napoleon in the same breath. Well, in Erik's case, you've canceled out the first element, but how about Napoleon?"

"He absolutely adored the man. Spoke about him all the time. Called him … let's see … 'The assailed lord and master'. Even wrote op-eds about him over and over."

"Okay, so we've covered Blue Baron and Napoleon. But you've also given us a clue as I'd call it … a clue regarding a person having a gripe against your husband."

"Yes. I don't understand 'clue', but gripe is correct."

"'Clue' means that Mr. Candido becomes a possible suspect in the murder."

"I get it."

"You know, Freda, it just dawned on me that we never explained why we came here."

"No, but it was pointed out to me by the police captain who called."

"I know, but so that we're completely on the same page, I'll summarize. We have the buying of the diamond; the reference to Napoleon; and a suspect in the murder. Let me just add that from here, we're going to Freetown and then to Brussels to conduct the same kind of research about similar murders there. I hope we're as successful as we've been so far, thanks to you."

"Coming up with two other suspects?"

"That will be part of it. So there'll be plenty to do and if you don't mind, we'll take our leave now. You've been most helpful."

"You won't join me for wine and dinner a little later? And the boys should be home soon."

"No, but thank you for the offer. We're not even staying around here overnight ... heading straight for Freetown. We'd like to do that one and then Brussels beginning tomorrow morning. So it's off to the airport. Maybe grab a sandwich or something there."

Their wait for a taxi didn't take long and during the ensuing ride, Paul phoned Otto to inform him of the information he'd garnered at Freda's home.

"A good start," Otto said. "Keep it up and continued good luck."

What's he driving at with "a good start." I started way before now.

Paul next decided to pass on the advice of Fritz and the histarians to visit the local police department. Instead, he called and learned there was no sensitive information to be offered. Thus, by the time they boarded the plane for Freetown, Paul felt he was up to date in his commitments.

And then came the call that would have rocked him back on his heels if he were standing.

"Hello, Paul? This is George Webley. Something horrible has happened since you called Otto. I was in his office going over some materials with him at the time. I left to get a document I forgot to bring up from my office, and then I heard a gunshot. It reminded me of when your Vincent was shot at. I rushed back upstairs and there he was on the floor."

"Don't tell me he was shot?"

"Shot and killed."

Chapter 8

The officer's ensuing answers did little to assuage either the deep sorrow or the fierce outrage that Paul felt. Later, he could barely recollect what was discussed with Webley, but later than that … when Paul had regained some sense of stability—one question stood out in his mind: could the killer have been the same guy who took a shot at Vincent? Paul thought he heard his blood flowing in the silence as he tried to get his arms around a logical answer. Under such circumstances, he and Vincent mutually agreed to shorten their stay in the next two cities. And Paul decided to forego any reading about Sierra Leone and Belgium or about their capital cities.

At the homes in those cities—Freetown and Brussels—they were courteous but almost detached, explaining away such conduct by alluding to Otto's death. The result of each visit, as it turned out, was a near-image of the one in Luanda, as both widows declared that certain men—Adam James, a travel agent and Victor Breitenbach, a factory worker—had longstanding beefs with their husbands. But neither woman knew why, and neither had much to say regarding Napoleon. Nonetheless, they left the homes by noon, satisfied with the knowledge that two more possible suspects had been identified.

Once inside Amsterdam's Park Plaza Hotel, having perspired the entire day and braving the tail end of a turbulent rain storm as they exited a taxi, Paul disregarded the gluey feel of wet clothing and dropped into an easy chair. Vincent went to the next room to dry off. Paul then contemplated various aspects of the past and how the immediate future might shape up. Early in his multifaceted career, he would not only think about problems that he had dealt with, but would enter them in a journal for safekeeping and potential further use. That was some time ago, however, and in more recent times, he would write down the situations that hadn't been experienced yet. The past versus the future. As it now stood, and not unexpectedly, there was a panoply of issues that still needed to be addressed. He wasn't stymied but was unsure of the order in which to proceed. And considering all concomitant emotions, he felt like a person trying to describe a keyboard without using his fingers. He had experienced   mental   anguish   during   past investigations, but it was never so intense. At least, he felt, he was caught up on sleep—for whenever he hadn't been, he tended to take on either too much in succeeding hours, or too many things at once. It was the latter that now gnawed at him, despite more than sufficient sleep. However, he wouldn't be deterred.

He joined Vincent in the next room, dried off, put on dry clothes, returned to the main room and sat at a desk. Happy to be rid of the stench of a wet shirt and of disengaging thoughts, he leaned down to his satchel and withdrew his hard-covered journal. He then began writing but not before reasoning once again that the act of transferring troubling thoughts to written words was therapeutic. Three obvious problems dominated the list. He wrote them down with some elaboration:

1—Locating the Blue Diamond. Helps find the killer. Some nations hope they can secure the diamond and use it as a bargaining chip for not being attacked.
2—Locating the killer.
3—Examining the area around Napoleon's sarcophagus in Paris.

Paul then referred to many previous entries and isolated notes in his bulging satchel and wrote down a second group, quite sure he was missing some things that needed consideration. It was a group of "must do" items and of pertinent questions:

> 1—Consult with *Vérité's* Cassell re the two
> members killed here in Amsterdam.
> 2—Consult with Cassell & Sophie re their
> blood relationship to Napoleon.
> 3—Attend Otto's wake, not his funeral.
> 4—Why was Bosnia given as last to visit?
> 5—Could some of my allies help out?
> Saltanban. Gomez. Fabio.
> 6—Could giving a lecture on Napoleon
> assist in any way?
> 7—So what about the suspects so far?

Once the entries were made, they were looked upon as though they were engraved in stone. Yet, still floundering around in his brain was a batch of disconnected details that he believed had to be separated out and faced head-on. It was a foggy batch, unidentifiable for the time being. He was used to this, however—to what others might have termed confusion. It wasn't that at all, for he understood the dynamics of his thinking, that the necessities of a proper and thorough criminal investigation included not only obvious steps to take but also ones that he couldn't see clearly until he moved further along. So he readjusted his thinking on travel when he once again understood what went with the turf before him. *What allows me to accomplish more ... traveling or phone calls?*

But he was never certain of the order in which to proceed. Nothing new. He would just go by the list in his journal, understanding that it wasn't the trains, taxis and rental cars that frustrated him, because they were a sine qua non for getting around. Rather, it was air travel that was at fault until he realized he had the JBCC from Hyannis at his disposal. And on a moment's notice. A plane that gave him plenty of time to sleep, study and organize.

He would have been delighted if the first two "must do" entries involved returning to the U.S., but Leon Cassell lived in Paris, and Paul was convinced that a visit there would be a temptation if not a distraction. He simply wasn't ready to confront the sarcophagus mystery. Besides, it was *last* among the first three problems listed. But a rational exception could be phoning Cassell, then flying to Brussels to see Sophie, then back to nearby Amsterdam—and he would still be on time for Otto's wake, which would probably take place on Friday or Saturday.

At about 1:30 p.m., he knew that Amsterdam and Paris were in the same time zone, so he placed a call to Cassell.

"Leon," he said, "we're through with the three cities. We came up with three possible suspects, so I'd say the travel was worthwhile."

Paul then indicated that Otto had been shot and killed and added that the tension was mounting.

"I never knew about him," Cassell said.

"Not a bad guy. Was the commissioner of the main police department around here. Ran it very efficiently. And all told, he gave me excellent advice."

"You think the murder has any relationship with what you're doing?"

"Can't figure it out yet. I hope not, but we'll see."

Paul was anxious to bring up the principle reason for the phone call and, while he would have liked to spend more time on the commissioner's fate, he switched abruptly to Napoleon.

"Leon, I know all about the fact you're related to the emperor. Plus the fact that Sophie Bauer is too. The DNA business and all that. We spent a lot of time on the subject, and to be perfectly frank, it's one of the reasons you and I get along so well. But that's neither here nor there. Is it alright if I ask you some questions about Napoleon and maybe even get a bit personal?

"Anytime, Paul. Anytime."

"Let's start with this: is that really his body in the sarcophagus? I'd rather call it a 'tomb'."

"Whose body?"

"Napoleon's."

"What tomb?"

"The one at the *Hôtel des Invalides.*"

"I assume so."

"I guess your entire family would know you and Napoleon are related, wouldn't they?"

"Yes, they do."

"So that means your children are related to him, too. Right? I mean your wife isn't because she's not a blood relative. Is my reasoning right?"

"Right again."

The more Paul spoke, the more pumped up he became and the more rapid the questioning, as if he had practiced a set drill beforehand.

"Do the *Invalides* people know about your DNA relationship with the emperor?" Paul asked.

"The higher-ups do, I'm sure. Like personnel from the *Préfecture de Police*."

"Now, just regarding the paintings nearby: their maintenance and safety would be under the jurisdiction of those higher-ups?"

"What's meant by 'nearby'?"

"Oh, somewhere around the tomb or upstairs in the gallery."

"Yes, their jurisdiction."

"Including replacing one, if they wanted to?"

"Yes."

"Well then, Leon, could you find out if one's been replaced within, say, the last year? They'd tell a Napoleon relative, I assume."

"I can try."

"And if one *has* been changed or altered in any way, how did it come about? I mean, did they just go ahead and do it on their own, or did someone request it—and if so, who?"

Leon's voice turned louder. "Wait a minute, Paul! What are you driving at with all this? I feel like I'm in a jury seat."

Paul apologized; a few more questions and answers took place; and then Leon said that much of his knowledge about *Invalides* and the sarcophagus came from their mutual friend, Guy Martin, a former journalist for the *Herald Tribune* in Paris.

"He's moved to your country, you know," Leon said. "Followed in your Vincent's footsteps at Harvard. He now teaches 'Journalism and Communications'."

"That's strange," Paul said. "Vincent never told me."

"Well, they're in separate buildings. He just started, so I suppose he never got around to looking him up yet."

Paul was as shocked to hear about that development as he was over his unplanned surge of questions. But he didn't let on.

"And Guy wants to see you, Paul. He told me so. We talk very often, and when we last did ... how ironic ... he hinted at something about Napoleon. I wasn't paying much attention at the time. But you must certainly know that he's a strong supporter of almost everything the man did in his day. I, myself, wouldn't go that far, but whatever.

And one other thing. I told him all about the Blue Baron, the apparent reason for the killings, and the other things you're handling. I hope you don't mind."

Paul withheld blinking for a few seconds before responding. "Not if it helps," he said. "And it will, won't it?"

"Well, it's one more person chipping in, so I hope it will."

Chapter 9

The flight to Boston seemed shorter than anticipated. Then there was a three-mile taxi ride to Harvard Yard. Before leaving Amsterdam, Vincent had phoned a friend at the university and learned that Guy Martin's office was located in Wadsworth House and that his single room there was officially labeled the Office for Scholarly Communication. Nearby were the massive Widener Library, the Memorial Church and University Hall.

Paul and Vincent showed up at the office around mid-day on Wednesday. They greeted one another warmly and Guy apologized for his "pint-sized" office, adding, "But I'm hardly here. Usually I'm teaching in a classroom."

The room was indeed tiny, but it appeared to have the basic essentials of desk, chairs, lamps, computer, printer, copier and a modest supply of books and journals.

Guy looked as if he hadn't aged since Paul last saw him two years before. Even his attire looked the same. He was a head shorter than Paul, with a puffy face that recessed his eyes and a ruddy nose that stood out against a pale complexion. His hair was obviously that of a toupee, contained no gray strands, and contrasted sharply with a thin silver-speckled mustache that was entirely appropriate for a man approaching sixty. He wore black, pleated trousers and a red bow tie over a yellow shirt rolled up at the sleeves, and the one thing most clear in Paul's memory was again before him: Guy's collection of pens and pencils stuffed into a plastic pocket protector.

Guy asked them to be seated in two wooden chairs in front of his matching desk. He sidestepped to the chair behind it and craned forward with arms bent before him, elbows resting on the desktop, hands folded beneath his chin.

"Okay, here you are. Thanks for making the trip, but I think it'll be worthwhile," Guy began, addressing Paul. "You do look the same, I must say. Your exploits must agree with you."

"Sometimes yes, sometimes no."

"What about this one?"

"Somewhere in the middle. And you look the same, too."

Not to be undone, Vincent said, "Excuse me, but how do I look, gentlemen?"

"We have to say the same. Right, Paul?"

"Right, but I see him all the time."

"So its three 'sames' in the same room," Vincent said and was not totally successful in concealing a smile.

Guy leaned back in his chair, stared at Paul and said, "Well, again I thank you for making the trip. Both Vincent there and I welcome you to Harvard; and good luck in your new job."

"I'll need it, I'm sure."

It didn't take long for Paul to grow impatient with the small talk. "Leon Cassell tells me you wanted to see me?" he queried.

"Yes, about Napoleon, his sarcophagus and a mysterious diamond. You know that I've studied his career endlessly and thought I knew it to the nth degree. But some developments I've come upon have taken me by surprise—and possibly will you, too. No one has written about them. Also, I hope you're aware that Leon has kept me abreast of your … your what? … your plight, I guess is the best way to put it."

"Yeah, I'm aware and it's fine with me. But I'm already in confusing territory. How did you find out about those developments?"

"It involves research in the last seven to ten days. What caught my attention was a report that the first slaves in your country didn't come from the West Indies as was originally thought."

"From where then?"

"From Angola! And according to Leon, that's a country you are ... or were ... dealing with."

Paul felt thick in the neck as he anticipated more daunting news. In a way, he didn't even want to hear about it.

"So," Guy continued, "I explored, I probed, I made inquiries, I followed trails, I read a long defunct publication called *The Napoleon Chronicle*. And what I found was that Napoleon was very fond of diamonds. He especially liked the one he referred to as 'The Blue King'. Get it? There was The Blue King and now we have the Blue Baron. It all stems from Napoleon. He worshipped that diamond, treated it like a religious stone. Whatever prayer he believed in, he said it while holding the diamond over his heart. He'd do the same whenever he had an audience to hear his aphorisms." Guy glanced at a pamphlet on his desk. "Like, 'A field of battle which the enemy has previously studied and reconnoitered should be avoided,' or 'March dispersed, fight concentrated,' or 'When it is possible to employ thunderbolts, their use should be preferred to that of a cannon,' or 'War is an immense art which comprises all others. It is also like politics, a matter of tact.' Then he'd kiss the diamond, never concerned about who was watching.

Imagine, Paul. This giant commander, worshipping a diamond through thick and thin."

Guy's long pause bothered Paul. "Go on. Please." he said.

"Next, we have the outright theft of Dagobert's Throne."

"Dagobert's throne? What the hell is that?"

"Some years ago, I was paid to find it. It's a replica of a bronze armchair of an original that belonged to a certain King Dagobert. Eventually I found that it wasn't missing at all—just misplaced. And add to that, that there were two so-called Fra Angelico paintings missing and that six ... yes, six ... of Napoleon's small paintings were also missing. It was discovered later that a certain enemy ... I don't know who ... replaced them with other paintings having tell-tale messages inside their back covers. And that he was found guilty of murdering six Napoleon allies."

"Wait! Hold it there. Could you tie this all together? What are you telling me?"

"Only this. But I shouldn't be using the word 'only' because it's more important than that, in view of what you're trying to accomplish. We have Napoleon; slaves originating from Angola; the Blue King diamond; the theft of Dagobert's Throne; missing Fra Angelico paintings; six of Napoleon's paintings missing—and I stress 'six'. Replaced by six others. I've pieced it all together and what I've come up with is that it all resembles your situation involving Napoleon; the painting around his sarcophagus; a missing special diamond, the Blue Baron; and the killing of six people. Here's my conclusion: if the killer liked Napoleon, he mimicked all of what transpired back in the early eighteen- hundreds. I mean, think of it: similar diamonds, six missing paintings, six persons killed, and so on. Did the killer pattern what he did after reading about the emperor and his misfortunes?"

"I see what you're driving at, Guy, but how does it help me?"

"In one important area: the painting near his sarcophagus. It suggests that it was stolen. If so, what's there now is a replacement. And if the thief went through that trouble, it's got to be examined, front and back. A message may reveal plenty. If the killer's behind all of this, and if he's a screwball, and he probably is, he might even have signed his name. So there's the Blue Baron, but you also have the killer's identity."

Even before this meeting with Guy, Paul had entertained the notion that a painting had been replaced, but not that any kind of message had been written. Each of the three gave the room a sweeping inspection as if they were being secretly monitored, but in so doing, each was implying that all that could have been said by either side had already been said.

Paul raised his sleeve to check his watch; he let the sleeve go; he then repeated the sequence.

"Time to leave, guys," he said, easing up from his chair.

"Can't I offer you some coffee here?" Guy asked hastily. "Or take you to dinner?"

"No, we've got to get going," Paul said. "But I'm extremely grateful for your helping out and even for considering to. Thank you so much."

"You're welcome, and I hope you succeed."

On the way out, Paul's mind wasn't made up yet on whether or not to take all of Guy's disclosures seriously.

Continue with what I've planned, or drop it all and go to Invalides? Drop it? No. Invalides? Later on, for there may not be a message there after all.

He played around with the disclosures before concluding that he wasn't minimizing what Guy had to offer, for it was interesting and, to a degree, some of it made good sense. But in the end, he considered the meeting like the second act of a two-act drama.

Such a consideration notwithstanding, they would continue with their schedule and, in the process, perhaps much of what Guy had shared with them might be either validated or dismissed.

Sophie Bauer was next. So it was a return to Brussels. Paul had been to her apartment once before to obtain a DNA sample that would substantiate her blood relationship to Napoleon. It was Paul, in fact, who coined the moniker of "lineage woman". As he remembered, there wasn't much else accomplished in calling on her then, but now, his seat-of-the-pants instinct told him the trip would be worthwhile. But why?

Chapter 10

B efore landing at Brussels Airport, Paul's last thoughts centered on the textbooks he'd written about European history. His first one was the initial installment of a series dealing with the region in and around Brussels, Belgium's capital city. He stated that it was one of the most important cities in northwestern Europe for two reasons: one, its location—along with neighboring Antwerp, Bruges and Ghent—smack in the middle of trading partners France, The Netherlands, Germany and, across the North Sea, the United Kingdom. He wrote about the peculiarity, as he characterized it, of the country's sharp division into the Dutch-speaking *Flemings* to the north and the French-speaking *Walloons* to the south.

The second reason and the one having greater impact on other major countries, including the United States, was the key role of Brussels in international politics and economics. For instance, headquarters for both the North Atlantic Treaty Organization and the European Union are located there.

Paul clearly recalled Sophie Bauer's neighborhood, which he had visited about two years before. Even the exact address: 2004 Muller Street. He had phoned ahead for permission to call on her and get her opinion about Napoleon diamonds and his sarcophagus. A taxi dropped him and Vincent off at a major intersection near an alley, which the driver identified as the designated street. And on the short walk to her apartment building, Paul deemed it odd that he was unconsciously recreating his behavior there last time. He scrutinized the few people they passed. None looked suspicious; none began stalking or tailing them; none regarded them with murderous intent. Once again, he felt relatively secure with the Stealth 9 mm at his ankle. But he had become so tired of interviewing people with a limited number of key questions and then, to be kind, extending the interview with meaningless conversation. He recognized that the important phase of investigations—not the travel but the investigations themselves—was the brief Q & A session that each necessitated. At least *his* sessions. He decided that, from this time forward, he'd ask his planned questions and then would "beat it", explaining that their schedule made it imperative to do so. He would therefore begin such an approach here with Sophie, leveling with her up front.

The sky was eerily dark, presaging an oncoming storm. She welcomed them into her small second-floor complex. It was airy and flower-laden with cheerful colors. She immediately asked if they'd like anything to eat or drink and they refused. They sat in the living room's grouping of three easy chairs and Paul was ebullient in his gratitude for her allowing the visit on such short notice. Rain pounding on a window made it good to be in there.

"Do be my guest whenever you wish, Paul. You know, most mid-sixty retirees don't receive many guests to begin with." She had a friendly, no nonsense "I can survive anything" manner.

"I have only three or four questions, Sophie, and then we're off. You may wonder why we aren't satisfied with a phone call. Well, it all stems from experience. Phone calls don't register answers in facial expressions and eyes, and I can't begin to tell you the number of times I've been misled by not witnessing them."

"You are thorough, I must say."

To continue on with his up-front prelude, Paul asked, "Do you know what the American idiom 'beat it' means?"

"To mix up, like for eggs and flour?"

"That too, but I'm driving at 'to hurry away'. Nothing bad intended, Sophie, but we have such a tight schedule that we'll be beating it very soon. Most of our investigations consist of a series of brief interviews with very little time spent on what I'd call fillers. I hope you understand."

"I do."

"So here we go." As usual, Paul produced a card and read from it. "We're aware that you're genetically related to Napoleon, just as Leon Cassell is. So because of that, have you been made more convinced about his love of diamonds?"

"Yes—plus by many sources I'd guess no one else is privy to."

"What's meant by many sources?"

"Oh, ancient letters, original manuscripts and so forth—things that were handed down. I have them locked up here."

"They're sources that no one else has?"

"Yes, except maybe Leon. He might have some, too. We never discuss it."

Paul let an opinion go, stripping details to the essentials. "So you'd say your knowledge of that—his love of diamonds—is more reliable than anyone else's, except possibly Leon's?"

"I'd say that."

"And in such a context, is there one diamond he particularly favored?"

"Yes, the Blue King diamond."

"Good. Now topic number two. Have you an opinion regarding any of the paintings near and about Napoleon's tomb at *Invalides*?"

"I've heard that one painting has been replaced, but I haven't any details."

"Who told you?"

"Leon."

"And a few more happenings. More current. The disappearance of a famous diamond, the Blue Baron; Napoleon's six stolen paintings; the killing of six people in this area and Africa. They're somehow related."

"What I've heard is that anyone who expresses a wish to buy it that diamond and mentions Napoleon's name at the same time could get killed."

"Correct. That, in fact, was the reason I was hired to travel around and interview nice people like you."

Paul then interpreted her eyes, telling him she wanted to ask her own question, for a change. "You know," she said, "it's funny you're here today, for just last week, I received a call from a woman named 'Marlene, the Diamond Queen'. We met two years ago. She was a big-time prostitute who just got out of prison in Buenos Aires. She often tried to get me to join her ranks. Imagine … a woman my age!"

"Still trying to enlist you?" Vincent asked, his first question.

"No, she wants me to handle her business activities. She's back to the same routine."

"I know about her plenty, but how did you meet?" Paul asked.

"She spent weeks throughout Brussels and Amsterdam. I bumped into her at a special school luncheon where she cornered all the men she could in our auditorium."

"Should I be seeing her, in your opinion?

"It wouldn't hurt. I'm told she was familiar with many dignitaries from different countries, including police department personnel. Men, of course. They say she performed day and night to keep everybody quiet, including the police. Maybe you could learn something from all that. She even boasted about you-know-what with all the pirates she could handle off the coast of Somalia. And how did she get paid? In diamonds at 500 dollars per. I hear that Eva Peron … Evita … also did some of that stuff for political reasons in Argentina. And she demanded diamonds too. Kept a box full of them. In the Pink House. You know, the one made famous in 'Don't Cry for Me, Argentina' in the balcony scene. The reason I'm bringing her into this is that Marlene wanted very badly to become a second Evita."

As Paul had predicted, flying back to confer with Sophie would prove to be most valuable. She had confirmed what Guy had offered regarding diamonds; regarding the sarcophagus and its nearby painting; regarding six stolen paintings belonging to Napoleon; and regarding six Napoleon allies who were murdered. Sophie also suggested visiting another person—in far-off Buenos Aires. *Would the Diamond Queen follow suit and also suggest another person?*

They made it to Amsterdam in plenty of time for Otto's wake. Outside the funeral parlor, Paul indicated the visit wouldn't take long. Vincent therefore decided to wait in the cab, so Paul went inside alone. He had been to many wakes on both sides of the Atlantic and always came away feeling the parlors looked alike, both inside and out.

This one, Cortlandt's, was located on a side street within the grounds of the Schiphol Airport and resembled a Gothic stone mansion from a distance, but up close, one could make out more wood than stone. Above a green awning which spanned the entire walkway from street to entrance, a keystone was etched with *Cortlandt's* in script. On either side, voussoirs were wedged between twin curves of dark hardwood, while a large Netherlands flag dangled in a concavity below. Inside, all was plush, fragrant and relatively muted aside from somber organ music pumping through speakers on four walls. After signing the guest book in the foyer, Paul walked slowly to the far end of a large receiving room and observed a short line of mourners standing before a closed casket surrounded by cascades of multicolored flowers. Bell-shaped, funnel forms, tubulars, butterfly-forms. Here and there, a half dozen husky men with wrinkle-free trousers and dark short-sleeved shirts stood against the walls like sentinels, their expressions frozen somber, their arms plastered with tattoos. Two of them had pistols attached to their belts.

To the right, quiet conversation droned from a receiving line where an older woman and two younger ones—no doubt Otto's relatives—either clasped hands with or hugged those who passed by. Behind the receiving line, a row of men and women sat stiffly; their mouths were turned down as if in unison. One of them was Officer Webley. After offering condolences to the three women, Paul circled around to Webley's backside and the officer rose from his chair. They shook hands.

"Sorry for your loss, George," Paul said.

"Not just mine. The whole department."

They chatted briefly about the friendliness and law enforcement capabilities of the Chief Commissioner. "He gave me such leeway," Webley said at one point. "He'll be sorely missed, that's for sure."

Paul decided to take his leave. The parlor's exit hallway was different from the way in, and when he was opposite an empty alcove containing many photographs of Amsterdam on the walls that were visible, he sauntered through its door. As he approached the far wall, he heard a click, spun around and saw that the door had been closed. He tried to open it and then realized it was locked! He searched for windows, found none, and then banged on the door. There was no response. *Trapped*!

Soon, the clatter of metal on metal resounded from a spot just below the doorknob. The door opened slowly and Paul stepped back. A mustachioed man, huskier than those he had seen in the receiving room, appeared in front of him. He was aiming a pearl-handled revolver at Paul's head, and as he came closer, his eyes watered with laughter as if he had finally found a lost treasure. The laugh proved to be a mistake, however, for the seconds it consumed were time enough for Paul to launch his karate maneuver and leg sweep. The gun swept across the alcove, bouncing off the far wall just as the man's body reached the floor. Paul ignored the groans, knowing that the man would survive, and he left the parlor in a hurry for fear that other assailants might show up.

Despite the harrowing experience, it didn't get lost on Paul that pearl-handled guns and mustaches could be traced to the three men at Elba's Volterraio's Castle; to the shooter at Vincent while at Otto's office; and now to a funeral parlor. This one bothered him the most.

Outside, he informed Vincent of the Cortlandt episode and received the following response: "See what happens when I'm not around?"

"So please be around."

The flight from Amsterdam to Buenos Aires was a projected 14 hours and Paul decided to break it up with a stopover in Falmouth to see Sylvie. It was a Saturday and she wouldn't be working. He phoned ahead to apprise her of his plans, including the fact that Vincent would be accompanying him and could stay over in one of their spare bedrooms. In a moment of self-pity just before the phone call, and despite his recent rationalization of extensive traveling, Paul exclaimed to himself: "All the phone calls; all the visits; all the interviews. Some positive, some negative. If only there were an easier way!"

But I asked for it and should have predicted it. Basically, though—aren't negative outcomes sometimes positive?

It had been nearly a week since he last saw Sylvie and, approaching their home, concluded he didn't miss her unless she was in his thoughts. And he thought about her every day. Their embrace was longer and stronger than last time—and speechless. Only Vincent uttered a sound: "Thanks so much for your hospitality."

Sylvie broke away and said, "What hospitality?"

"Putting me up."

"But hospitality is for strangers and you're certainly not one of them."

Vincent repeated his thanks.

Paul rubbed his shoulders as if they hurt. Then while they took chairs in the kitchen, he said, "We're leaving for Buenos Aires in the morning, but I'll bring you up to date. It's been nearly a week, you know."

"Not to say I haven't been curious, my dear. 'Worried' is more appropriate."

"I understand and I'm sorry. Everything went so fast. It's almost like being whipped while running a marathon with no end in sight."

"So be it. But why Buenos Aires?"

"To see—of all people—Marlene Kessler."

Sylvie wiggled around to fortify herself in her chair. "Marlene the Diamond Queen? Now I've heard it all!"

"So did I when she dropped her name."

"Who's 'she'?"

"Sophie Bauer. He had so much to say. Let's have something to eat and I'll go through it for you. I'll help with the meal—just sandwiches will do."

"No, no. You both sit and I'll handle it. Boiled ham all right?"

"Anything," Paul said. "And maybe some lemonade or soda."

Vincent nodded.

Lunch went fast, Paul managing to chew while summarizing the activities of the past six days and not in order but as they flowed through his mind: Fritz's recommendations of places to visit; learning of the men who had gripes against the victims in their cities; consulting with Freda Hoek, Sophie Bauer and the two widows in Freetown and Brussels; Otto Bleeker's murder; the conclusions of Guy Martin; the wake at Cortlandts Parlor. He was certain he'd accidentally left out some details, but it was no accident that he failed to mention the attacks on his life.

"But why travel all the way to Argentina to see that prostitute?" Sylvie asked.

"Sophie Bauer recommended it. She got a call from Marlene about being her business manager, but I think Sophie thought there was more to it than that, and that I should investigate. The other reason for going is to revisit the Pink House to see if Evita's diamond box is there after all. This may qualify as a wild goose chase, but you know me and my thoroughness."

"Oh, do I ever. And one final point that's been disturbing me: Is all this traveling necessary?"

"Not 100 per cent, I suppose. It could be confusing, but the whole purpose of most visits is primarily to identify possible suspects in the six murders … as I said before … the whole 'gripes' thing. So far we have three possible suspects, and when I get to the two *Vérité* families in Amsterdam, there may be two more. We'll see."

Chapter 11

O n the way to Buenos Aires, Paul couldn't help but think about the many times he and the city's police chief, Joe Gomez, had collaborated on criminal investigations. Though not recently. Yet, the chief was his favorite and most trustworthy official in all the South American cities. In addition to Argentina, Paul had investigated cases in nearly every country: Brazil, Colombia, Venezuela, Paraguay, Ecuador, Peru, and even in the Tierra del Fuego archipelago of Southern Chile.

He well remembered Argentina's history as often presented to him by the chief. Eva Peron had coordinated a network for helping Nazis relocate throughout her country after World War II. Tangential damage had occurred to Switzerland's banking industry due to its collaboration with Adolph Hitler. And financial manipulations involving Hitler's Jewish victims secretly took place in Argentina. But Paul wasn't there to research any of that. Marlene and any information she could provide ... relative to his overall assignment ... these were what he was after. Otherwise he wouldn't have made the journey.

At this stage of most assignments, Paul began referring to heads-up phone calls as "necessary evils". He made one to Gomez during the flight, fairly confident that the chief would be available on a moment's notice—and on any day.

"Anxious to see you, Joe. It's been much too long."

"Well I'll be ... all okay?"

"All okay, and I plan on arriving at my home-away-from-home at about three."

"Today, I hope?"

"But it's a Sunday. Actually I'm surprised I reached you at your office. Will it ruin your schedule if we drop by— say at about three-thirty? Vincent's with me."

"Ruin? Never. You're both always welcome even without a prior call. Vincent's well, too?"

"Yeah, and still the best."

"But what's on your mind?"

"You'd never guess, so I'll toss you a name: Marlene Kessler."

"Marlene? You mean the Diamond Queen?"

Paul pictured Gomez tumbling from his chair. "That's the one. She may be able to help me in my current job. I assume she's out of prison by now."

"Paul, I haven't thought about her in some time but, speaking of jobs ... do you know what she's doing?"

"Haven't the faintest."

"Back to her same old tricks, I hear. And I mean tricks for what it stands for in her world. Of course, prostitution is legal in our city, and what she does elsewhere isn't checked out."

Ever since he met Gomez some ten years or so ago, Paul was impressed with his command of the English language and often congratulated him on how much of it he learned by spending six years in the States and graduating from a community college in upstate New York.

"I'd like to talk to her, Joe. Can you arrange it?"

"What I'll do is contact her parole officer and we'll go from there. By the time you arrive, I hope to have it arranged. Maybe not for today, but is tomorrow all right?"

"We'll stay as long as it takes. And later— when we get to your office—I'll explain what this is all about. For now I'll just say I've taken on a job and may have gotten in deeper than I expected."

In the expansive police department building, Paul and Vincent navigated their way to the chief's private office. There, after earnest greetings, the three men began reminiscing even before taking seats opposite one another.

Paul looked Gomez over and asked, "You been taking some fountain of youth medicine?"

"Very kind ... very kind," Gomez replied.

He was decked out in his usual uniform but had more gold and silver badges than Paul remembered from his last trip there. Tall, trim and slightly grayer at the temples, to Paul he still looked and spoke more like a Brooklynite than a South American. He indicated that the parole officer had settled the Marlene meeting. She was in the area and would be there at ten in the morning.

Paul said he was delighted and then didn't waste words as he outlined his current responsibilities. "They range from identifying the killer of six individuals in foreign countries, to the role of diamonds and Napoleon, to the sarcophagus at *Invalides*. Of special meaning for my visit here is information given to me by Sophie Bauer, who happens to be a blood relative of no other than ... Napoleon."

"Which was?" the chief inquired. "I mean, the information."

"She said Marlene wants her to handle her business activities throughout Amsterdam and Brussels. You know what those activities are. I suppose she meant scheduling. The gal doesn't have time to do her *own* scheduling? C'mon."

"Once a courtesan, always a courtesan," Gomez said. "No time for details."

"Two things really caught my attention, though," Paul continued. "One concerned her contact with so-called dignitaries from around the world, and also with pirates. They get around, as you well know ... branching out from the Somalia area. Branching *way* out. Sophie claimed the dignitaries and pirates might be of some help to me. Can you imagine? The other thing—and this really surprised me—is that she brought up the Pink House and Evita' s diamond box. We never found it before, but I'd like to have another look, Joe."

"We can do that ... sure. You want to go now?"

"Love to. Good ... means we'll have it done before tomorrow's meeting."

The drive to the Casa Rosado—the Pink House—took less than five minutes. It seemed that all traffic had moved aside to make way for Gomez's police car, even though he had no siren blaring. They pulled into a rear parking lot as they had done two years before and began walking toward a rear entrance.

"Sure brings back memories, Joe," Paul said. "You have a key?"

"Yes, but I've never used it since you were here last. I'll bet there are still some cobwebs across the door." The chief fumbled through a ring of keys until he found the right one.

"Still means a long time. Could be there are recent webs," Paul said.

"How's that? Say, that reminds me about your mentioning you've made a study of cobwebs. Sounded like it when you gave your little explanation of the various kinds. Fascinating. Could you go through it again?"

At the door, two thin cobwebs spanned its width. Gomez delayed inserting the key, leaned against a brick supporting column and repeated his last question.

"Glad to," Paul said. "First off, they're all made by spiders, but dust comes into the picture, too. Any web is made up of short irregular strands arranged haphazardly and because the strands are sticky, they gather dust. One of the most common—at least in the U.S.—is the one made by black widows. Then we have the cellar spider, which makes loose ones in dark places. Not too much dust. And the jumping spider. It trails what's called a single filament dragline wherever it crawls and never makes a real web.

"Now if webs are crisscrossed, no one's disturbed them for a long time. If they're just a strand or two, they could have been created recently."

Gomez straightened up and broke the two thin strands with his finger.

"Those could be relatively recent," Paul said.

"What's recent mean?" Gomez asked.

"Oh, ten minutes and up to two or three months."

"But not two years."

"No, not that long."

"Thanks, Paul. That's two times. I'll remember it well." He opened the door and they walked into a dimly-lit room. All shades were drawn, lights were out and the room smelled of must. The chief turned on the lights. Off to the side, a table with a large carton labeled *Eva's Personal Effects* in Spanish was still there. Paul opened it and sifted through the same collection of items as before: cosmetics, silverware, candles, photographs, medals, epaulets, books, folded articles of clothing.

"No box," Paul said disgustedly.

"Spread open the clothing," Vincent said.

Paul unfolded three layers and then inhaled and gasped practically at the same time. "Here it is!" he said. "Excellent, Vincent!"

"Sure is," Gomez said.

It was a deep, elongated silver box made of metal, and was not locked. Paul opened it carefully, as if expecting something to fly out. It was filled with at least 50 diamonds—all round, shiny and cut to about half-an-inch in diameter. They reminded Paul of those he had seen Gomez remove from

Marlene's concealed belongings on her first day in prison.

"So, that's that," Paul said. "A good score, so far."

"I'm happy for you, Paul," Gomez said.

Paul and Vincent spent the night at their usual Park Plaza Hotel, both falling off to sleep with no difficulty.

Marlene was already sitting in the chief's office when the three men marched in at nine-fifty-five a.m. They had spent half an hour in the cafeteria having a light breakfast.

She was touching up her face while fussing with a small, round mirror. Very attractive and curvaceous, she appeared to be in her mid-thirties and was stylishly attired in tight-fitting charcoal slacks, a similarly colored tight jersey and gladiator sandals. Around her neck was a turquoise necklace with sterling silver settings, while around her wrist was a brass cuff bracelet of rose quartz and moonstone. Jet black hair was pulled back in a chignon and her smile seemed tantalizing if not beckoning.

No words were exchanged as she ran her eyes over the three men. Then she broke the silence: "My-oh-my, three guys who never experienced my services."

Only Gomez responded: "Too expensive."

"We could have negotiated," she said.

She stood up and planted a shallow kiss on their cheeks.

"We meet again, Marlene," Paul said. "And I couldn't help but notice you carry no purse. Where do you keep that mirror?"

"In my breast pocket. Sometimes I need it fast for … for … for positioning."

"Heck," Vincent said, "I might as well get in on this. So your top stays on?"

"Please, gentlemen," she said. "That's enough of that. How can I help?"

What with all her traveling, Paul doubted he'd have this opportunity again, so he plunged right into some questions he'd planned on eventually asking.

"We recently visited with Sophie Bauer, who recommended we also visit with you. She mentioned you've … ah … met with dignitaries in quite a number of cities. Do you remember any of them?"

"The cities or the men?"

"The men."

"No, I wouldn't recognize their names if you quoted them to me. And they all acted the same."

"Pirates then, do you … ."

"They were all the same, and I don't know any names."

"So it would be accurate of me to say that all your liaisons involved men who were anonymous to you?"

"Yes, anonymous."

"Ordinary businessmen and the police?"

"Both."

"And pirates."

"Some."

"And it will continue to be that way—all secretive?"

"Yes. Then no one gets hurt or worries about getting hurt."

Paul wanted to have her think he wasn't prepared for the interview, but he knew exactly how to proceed. He'd learned the approach by observing attorneys in many courtrooms, trying to win over the jurors by building their cases as if ad libbing.

"On another subject, Marlene. We went to the Pink House yesterday and found Evita's box of diamonds. Loads of them. Am I correct in assuming, therefore, that she did what you do? Only part-time versus full-time?"

"I confess I wanted to mimic her. She's responsible for my conduct, top to bottom. Even now, I want to be like her. I want to walk in her footsteps."

Marlene's answers had become wrapped in emotion. *Has a nerve been struck?*

"Just one more question and we have to leave," Paul said. "You've been most cooperative."

"I have a question for you after you finish, Paul. Okay with that?"

"Certainly. But first, here's my last one. If you want to be like a diamond-loving Evita, can some man want to be like a diamond-loving Napoleon?"

"Napoleon? Why him?"

"Hypothetical. I've been told he liked diamonds. You've heard of the Blue Baron?"

"Yes. A man mentioned it. In fact, every time we got together, he did. That was, maybe, five times."

Paul let the revelation slide. "Well," he said, "Napoleon treasured the Blue King, and the Baron may be a facsimile of it. But let's get to your question."

"Yes. Why is all this important to you?"

"I won't go into detail, but I've been retained to help solve some murders—six of them. Diamonds and Napoleon have become important in the solution."

On the return drive to Gomez's office, Paul thanked him for not entering the question and answer session.

"You're welcome. I felt I'd only confuse matters. You handled it well. Drew her out before she even recognized it."

Paul decided to level with the chief. "I'm entertaining the idea that some person wants to imitate Napoleon. I've had an inkling—even before going to the Pink House— that such imitating is not being unusual of Napoleon or anyone. To me, both were confirmed when we saw Evita's diamonds. By both, I mean 'imitating Napoleon' and 'not being unusual'. My last thought at the Pink House was that Marlene was imitating or mimicking Evita. The sex life and being paid in diamonds."

Paul and Vincent spent no further time in Buenos Aires, turning down Gomez's offer to stay for lunch, or even dinner. But Paul assured him he'd be kept informed.

During the flight to Amsterdam, Paul figured his agenda called for him to check out another of Sophie's references: pirates. He thought that doing so was overkill, but if he didn't, it could have been similar to past omissions, ones that later proved crucial to his solving of a case or of locating a missing treasure. One time, he didn't follow up on something he considered minor but later it proved to be significant. He then dreamed up an algorithm and had stuck by it ever since: To prevent defeat, be *complete.*

Whenever "pirate" popped up in his mind, so did "Mafia". And whenever "Mafia" did, so did "Fabio." That was Fabio Calderone, who lived in Calabria, at the most southern tip of Italy. Thanks to him, Paul had developed a harmonious relationship with gangsters around the world, even with the notorious Ndrangheta and the picciotti d'onore. Fabio had made clear that all gangs looked upon Paul favorably because he had always leveled with him about certain peoples and countries. And Fabio did the same. Sylvie, however, was leery about underworld figures in general. She often voiced concerns about Paul's dealing with them, prompting him to say, "Remember, dear ... there are bad gangsters and good gangsters." Her comeback was: "Thank God Fabio's a good one." The last time this repartee took place, Paul reminded her of Fabio's role in assisting him and a committee of friends in preventing a worldwide sarin attack, one that would have destroyed mankind.

A phone call to Fabio was in order. But first he wanted to brush up on pirates, so he withdrew an account of them that he'd stored in his satchel years ago. He finally admitted to himself that the bulging satchel was his own miniature library.

Piracy has changed drastically. There is the old fashioned kind and the new fashioned kind. Modern pirates today are definitely part of organized crime gangs that target cargo vessels and even cruise ships and private yachts. Seaborne piracy against transport vessels remains a significant issue, with estimated worldwide losses of 16 billion U.S. dollars per year, particularly between the Red Sea, off the coast of Somalia, and also in the Strait of Malacca and Singapore—which are used by over 50,000 commercial ships a year.

Modern pirates favor small boats and take advantage of the small number of crew members on modern cargo vessels. They also use large vessels of their own to supply the smaller boarding vessels. Moderm pirates can be successful because a large amount of international commerce occurs via shipping. Major shipping routes take cargo ships through narrow bodies of water such as the Gulf of Men and the Strait of Malacca, making them vulnerable to being overtaken and boarded by small motorboats. As usage increases, many of these ships have to lower speeds to allow for navigation and traffic control, making them prime targets for piracy.

Also, pirates often operate in regions of developing or struggling countries with smaller navies and large trade routes. Pirates sometimes evade capture by sailing into waters controlled by their pursuer's enemies. With the end of the Cold War, navies have decreased in size and patrol less frequently, while trade has increased, making organized piracy far easier.

Modern pirates are sometimes linked with organized crime syndicates.

Paul stopped short of reading on, for he wasn't really interested in what he'd read thus far, except for the last line of the article.

Even that didn't satisfy him. He was looking for a notation that pirates were often associated with business dignitaries—and he would integrate that with Marlene's widespread activities. He admitted it was farfetched but he wondered if pirates—as well as legitimate dignitaries—could provide a sliver of information about prostitution, diamonds and the six murders. And even go so far as to naming some names.

Marlene had said she didn't know the names of her clients, but perhaps pirates would be proud to name themselves. *And I could follow through with interrogating them.*

Paul made the call to Fabio—once again on the plane—when the estimated time in Italy was around six p.m.

"Hey, paisano," Paul said. "It's me, Paul."

"Va. Bene. How's it going?"

"Fine. And you? Still barbering?"

"Part-time that and part-time at the meat packing place."

"You know, I never asked you. What do you do there?"

"I cut up slabs of meat before they're packed."

"Oh, so you cut hair and you cut meat."

Fabio laughed through his next comment: "That's about right."

"Hope you don't ever cut up humans," Paul said.

"Never. That's for my Mob friends."

Paul didn't care for and didn't know how they'd wandered into such a subject. He switched it.

"Why I'm calling, Fabio, is to ask if you know of any pirate friends who've feasted on a gal named Marlene?"

"The Marlene from before?"

"That's the one."

"She's still at it?"

"That's what I hear. All over the place."

"So you're asking about pirates feasting on *her* meat?"

"Fabio!"

"Sorry. I got lost there. But what I can do is call the head of some of the Mob families in Europe and find out. Then I'll give you a call."

"Perfect!"

They reviewed old times and promised to visit one another in their respective countries. Paul ended the conversation with a poorly enunciated, "Grazie and buon giorno."

As he leaned back and tried to relax, he thought of the remaining family visits ahead. And the "goddamn" phone calls that went with them. It had gotten to the stage where looking in on *Invalides* kept getting pushed nearer to the end of his priorities. Was he afraid of what he might find there? What would he rather have on his mind? More about Napoleon would do the trick, so he decided on a stopover in Paris to confer with one of his two Brasserie Lipp buddies, Maurice Delacroix, an expert on Napoleonic military exploits. He had already spent time with the other one: Guy Martin who had since moved to Harvard Square. Paul knew that a subsequent ride from Paris to Amsterdam on the Thalys Bullet train would take about three hours. He knew because he had ridden it before.

Much like introducing a section into a novel that slows its action, he believed that such a diversionary visit would slow the action of his investigation and all that went with it. But he concluded it was just what he needed in the face of hurried travel, constant phone calls, and a steady stream of interviews. He felt that doing so was not to receive what Maurice might have to offer as advice but to hear his thoughts about Napoleon's tactics on the battlefield. Paul had heard him go on-and-on about them several times in the past and, despite the repetition, he was always enlightened. And entertained.

He consulted his worn-out address book, located Maurice's home phone number and called him. The result was filled with warm regards and, "Yes, Paul, I still go there. Usual time, usual table."

The three men had frequently shared experiences over lunch at the Lipp Restaurant, which was made famous by Ernest Hemingway and his preference for that one over several others in the vicinity. It opened in the late 1800s during the Franco-Prussian War and had grown to be known among the 12,000 Parisian *cafés* as the best place to "eat and meet", having won the Legion of Honor in 1958, commemorating that distinction. Paul always made sure to come by at no later than 11:30 a.m.—when they had promised one another they would place their orders. Even though this was two years later, he would not break that promise.

Chapter 12

They arrived at Paris' Charles de Gaulle Airport at two on Tuesday morning. They hailed a cab and on the drive to their usual hotel, the Meridian Montparnasse, it finally dawned on Paul that they would be passing by the *Hôtel des Invalides*. He tossed it from his mind after assuring himself that he was not ready to enter it until maybe a few days later. That he'd have to bone up on possible reactions to what he might discover around the sarcophagus. The taxi drove onto the Malakoff Highway in the direction of the Eiffel Tower, then slowed down along the Avenue de la Grande *Armée*, through the Arc de Triomphe, onto the *Champs Élysées* and over the Pont de la Concorde. When Paul noticed the *Hôtel des Invalides*, he shut his eyes for a moment.

It had been about a year since Paul had stayed at the Montparnasse and, as before, it barely met his expectations, causing him to wonder why he kept choosing that particular hotel. He had no answer except he liked the fact that it clashed with all the neoclassic structures merely blocks away. None of which he favored.

Inside, the lobby decor was in pastels. There was a reservation counter that spanned an entire wall, archways to two cocktail lounges behind two other walls, bronze statues of war heroes at every corner, contemporary furnishings and light fixtures, an overuse of mirrors and glass and, even at that hour, background music from America's Broadway. The lobby was empty of guests, but four women employees were busying themselves behind the counter. On what, Paul couldn't figure.

They registered, were assigned to a 12th floor room and found it clean and serviceable. Paul was disappointed that its view contained none of the well-known icons of Paris, but he reminded himself that he was not there to see the sights but for a different purpose.

At eleven a.m., with Vincent nearby, Paul phoned Leon Cassell to inform him of what had taken place in Buenos Aires and to request his calling the two *Vérité* families about a possible visit the next day, along with directions to their homes. Leon agreed to do so and was to call Paul back when that was accomplished.

After hanging up the phone, Paul reached out to shake Vincent's hand in ostensible triumph and exclaimed, "I can't believe it! Someone else making arrival calls for me!"

Vincent had no comment on that, but announced that he'd decided not to accompany Paul to the Lipp. "You won't believe it, Paul, and you didn't notice because you were having plenty of sleep on the plane, but I was wide awake for a good part of the time. So I'm going back to bed. Besides, you need the talk with Maurice more than I do." Paul made an exaggerated sign-of-the-cross.

When he entered the restaurant at 11:25, he sauntered along one of its lateral walls at the same time Maurice came in through a side entrance. He was still using a cane clumsily and Paul nearly tripped over it. He stepped back to get a good view of him and then they both fumbled through a handshake and embrace.

"It's been a long time," Maurice said.

"Too long. You doing well, I hope?"

"Well enough for an old man."

"But with a lot of old memories."

The Lipp's odors, sounds and ambience hadn't changed in the two years since Paul had last been there. Mustard and onion aromas were the same. Edith Piaf music was the same. The plaque displayed under its outside awning was the same. It was written in both French and English.

ON THIS SPOT, ERNEST HEMINGWAY
WROTE:

The beer was very cold and wonderful to drink. The pommes a l'huile were firm and marinated and the olive oil delicious. I ground black pepper over the potatoes and moistened the bread in the olive oil. After the first heavy draft of beer, I drank and ate very slowly. When the pommes a l'huile were gone, I ordered another serving of cervelat. This was a sausage like a heavy, wide frankfurter split in two and covered with a special mustard sauce. I mopped up all the oil and all of the sauce with bread and drank the beer slowly until it began to lose its coldness. I finished it and ordered a demi ...

They took seats on the same art deco chairs they pulled out from behind a small table overflowing with magazines. Their covers touted Parisian cuisine and nightlife. Like Hemingway, they both ordered cervelat and beer.

Suddenly Paul's smartphone vibrated at his hip. "Excuse me," he said to Maurice, reflecting on who might be calling—Fabio or Leon. It was Fabio.

"I've got the answer," he said. "Many, many and I mean many have known that Marlene gal for years."

"By many, you mean pirates."

"Yes, pirates. But not only that. When they were sneaking onto cargo ships, she would tag along as bait."

"Bait for what?"

"For allowing them to board the ship. And get this, Paul. They would already have auctioned her off ahead of time. I mean to be screwed. They even had fights over it. And the longer they stayed to steal money from the ship's crew, the more times she got screwed on the ship."

Paul looked up at Maurice, glad that he hadn't been in on the conversation. *If it nauseated me, I can't imagine what it would have done to a much older man.*

He had heard enough, worded it that way to Fabio, and thanked him for the research.

"I'll have to question some pirates one of these days," Paul said. "Maybe they befriended some prominent men in their travels."

Paul then detailed the importance of any pirate or businessman association and how it could impact on diamonds and the murder solution. He visualized Fabio's facial expression through the brief silence that ensued.

"Thank you again," he said.

"You're very welcome," Fabio said, "And I'm glad it's you handling all of this and not me."

After indicating they'd keep in touch and exchanging Godspeeds, Paul nearly missed slipping the phone onto his belt. He still couldn't believe the extent to which Marlene had surrendered her body. Granted Evita was no saint, but how could Marlene even think about following in her footsteps?

Paul returned his attention to Maurice. "Sorry about that," he said, "It was a call I was expecting, but not the news."

"Good or bad?"

"Depends." Paul chose not to elaborate, instead forcing himself to think up a way to combine humor and sincerity in his next statement. "For an old geezer like you," he said, "you look like I hope to when I reach your age." In the back of his mind, however, there was a different ending: "*If* I reach your age."

Maurice was a seventy-something, slender man who obviously tried to hide a tendency to stoop. The incoordination with his cane was the result of a fine hand tremor and failing eyesight, and his intellectual prowess had a chink or two. He was wearing a black beret with some kind of faded medal at its front edge; both suspenders and a belt; and a light blue shirt under a darker blue jacket. There still was no smile, little trace of his teeth and a facial grayness that reminded Paul of the facades at Fontainebleau Palace.

While devouring their meal, Paul said, "I'd like to get your views of Napoleon again. I'm writing another book about him and the more I can learn, the better." It was a lie but an innocuous one. He simply wanted to get lost in Maurice's rhetoric. He knew what was coming up, as he had during other occasions there with the retired army general. Paul had marveled at his word-for-word description of the emperor's military history as well as his own. And he had never tired of the repetition.

"If you insist," Maurice said. "I'll eventually get to the 'asking, answering and amplifying' you've heard me cover before. And my apologies ahead of time. I'm afraid I usually come on rather strong. Some people call me brassy. Not a bad term really. Reminds me of trombones and trumpets."

Paul thought, *"Ah, the trombones and trumpets once more."*

"I realize you've heard most of this before and probably enjoy hearing it—over and over—or you wouldn't be here. Fact is, I enjoy delivering it, too. Over and over.

"So continuing on. 'Asking, answering and amplifying'—the triple 'A's'—is an old military slogan I often used for troops under my command—and you certainly aren't under my command, Paul, so please forgive me."

For now, Paul chose not to comment because he was eager to become absorbed in what lay ahead.

"But first, I want to begin a different way—I mean to the way you're used to hearing. I continue to hold that Napoleon was murdered. There's reason to believe ... and I, for one, believe it ... that he was poisoned by arsenic long before he arrived at St. Helena."

This time, Paul couldn't resist. "What reason?" he asked.

"Examine the battles," Maurice said.

"*Here it comes*," Paul thought. "*And I'll play along.*"

"I wouldn't want to prejudice your own analysis, but as long as you asked for the reason, you know that the prevailing theory these days is that Napoleon was poisoned by arsenic and you no doubt realize that it can be administered in small doses over a long period of time."

"Yes, but the relevance to the military battles?"

"His behavior during the last of them, his judgment being erratic, his mental state. Once the poisoning began to take hold, he made error after error. Some of the things he did, or didn't do, would have been unheard of in his earlier campaigns. Take the Russian campaign. Eighteen-twelve. Errors you'd never expect. And why? You'll see. You'll put it all together. But please, don't waste time on what he *did*; look at what he *didn't* do. The brilliant 'diamond-shaped' formation ...1806, against Prussia; his 'spider web' tactic; his 'square battalion'; his 'envelopment attack'. What happened to them? Abandoned for what purpose? Defeat? I commend you for your books—very well researched, very well written. But you didn't analyze with an eye that some outside force was influencing Napoleon. Like poison. He has his admirers—me, for one—and his detractors, I'll admit, but along with Alexander he must be considered the greatest military leader of all time, and as I said, some of his last battlefield decisions were way out of character."

Paul was surprised at a sudden lapse in the conversation and leaped to take advantage of it. "You game for a question or two, Maurice?" he asked.

"Certainly."

"You know my background. Can you repeat some parts of yours?"

"Love to. As Cicero said, 'Gallia est omnis divisa in partes tres.' All Gaul is divided into three parts. The same with my career: all of it military. The first part? Twenty-six years in the Foreign Legion. Became Colonel. Indochina, Africa, others. The second part: teacher at the Special Military School of St. Cyr for ten years. Became General. Our motto was, *'Ils s'instruisent pour vaincre.'* They study to vanquish. You might be interested to know that Napoleon founded the school in eighteen-two. It's where Charles de Gaulle went. Then the third part: with Gendarmerie Nationale right up to four years ago. That's our national police force. Mainly participated in ceremonies involving foreign heads of states or governments. Another way of looking at my background, my life, if you will, is to divide it into necessary pursuits and voluntary pursuits, although 'necessary' and 'voluntary' can be interchanged. But for now I won't go into that except to say that my main voluntary pursuit was to study the Napoleonic Wars. That I have gladly done since I was a young boy. And I've written regularly—not big volumes. No patience for that anymore, just some articles, commentaries, for my favorite organizations: The Dutch Line Infantry Battalion, the French Line Infantry Battalion, Supporters of the Waterloo Battlefield, The European Napoleonic Society. You might find these groups useful someday."

Paul said, "And you spent some time in the United States I'm told. Where and how long?"

"I suppose you might say I was on loan to your West Point Academy: a visiting lecturer in residence for four years. Went so fast ... one of the highlights of my life."

Paul checked his watch. "This went so fast, too, and I thank you."

Maurice reached for his cane before rising.

Paul had received more than he wanted. Almost like a trip to never-never land. He explained it that way to Vincent, who apparently hadn't needed as long a nap as he'd thought. He was watching T.V. back in their hotel room when Paul walked in.

"It went well then?" Vincent asked.

Paul nodded.

"Gave you some relief and made this stopover worthwhile?"

"Yes and yes."

Chapter 13

Midway on the Thalys train to Amsterdam, Leon's call came through.

"The *Vérité* families are looking forward to your visits with them this afternoon," he said. "I explained your role in working for *Vérité* and all about the rounds you're making. One of these families is headed up by an electrician's wife. The other victim—an accountant—wasn't married but had a brother who'd like to talk to you."

"Nice job, Leon. How about their addresses?"

"They said that many cabs have been to their homes lately, all with mourners over their losses. And that they lived fairly close to one another, so you shouldn't have a problem. I don't know if you remember their names, but they're Willem

Frelinghuyens and Jules Mulder. Both were very loyal to *Vérité.*"

Paul rang the bell at the Frelinghuyens' six-room Ranch and when he heard, "Come right in," he allowed Vincent to enter first. A young woman met them in the vestibule and shook their outstretched hands. She began to cry.

"Sorry," Paul said. "Is everything all right?"

"Yes ... yes. I'm the one who should be sorry, but anything or anyone who reminds me of Willem's passing brings on the tears." She dried her eyes with a tissue.

She appeared to be about thirty, with full-bodied brown hair arranged in spliced long layers. Her moist green eyes complemented her hair color and roamed despondently between Paul and Vincent. She was dressed in a black blouse and matching slacks. Before leading the way into a den, Paul thought that her smile was improvised. He also sized her up as a raving beauty who was still suffering.

They sat at a table rimmed with three glasses, a pitcher, and a plate of assorted cookies. "Do help yourselves," she said. "The pitcher has lemonade, but I can fetch you something stronger."

They both declined. Under the circumstances, it was the last thing Paul was interested in. He harked back to how he felt during the previous family visits and classified his current feelings as being identical: uncomfortable ... tense ... out of place.

"Thank you for receiving us at a most difficult time," he said, "but we won't stay more than a few minutes, Mrs. ..."

"No, no," she said, interrupting him. "My first name is Catherina—Cath for short. Do use it. The last is too difficult to pronounce— Frelinghuyens. Also, I can't wait to get something off my chest, but you go first."

"And we go by Paul and Vincent. You're not immune to a few questions then?"

"Not at all."

"Okay. Have you communicated with the other five victims' families?"

"Yes, we've kept in touch. The police have suggested it."

"So by now, you probably know the kinds of questions I'll be asking."

"I think so. But do go ahead. I'll answer almost anything."

Paul began to feel somewhat at home. "Your husband was an electrician?" he asked.

"Yes."

"Worked alone or within a company?"

"Within a company. 'Amsterdam Works'."

"Many employees?"

"About a hundred. They weren't all electricians, though."

"And to your knowledge, he got along with them?"

"Very much so. So much that he was recently elected publicity chairman of the 'Works'. That's what it went by: the 'Works'."

She raised one hand in a "stop" position. "This might be a good time to bring up what's been troubling me. It may involve Willem's murderer. Two days before he was killed, he received a phone call from a man who said he didn't like what *Vérité* stood for. He said it had to do with … who knows, because the phone went dead."

Paul underlined what took three seconds to scratch onto his pad. "As you can see, we're taking notes. Hope you don't mind."

"Not at all. Do you think that's important? I mean the phone call."

"Could be. It might be considered in with the gripes certain people had with those who were killed." Paul pointed to his pad. As did Vincent.

"I'd like to change the subject … uh … Cath. The police—or somebody—no doubt told you about the Blue Baron and Napoleon?"

"Yes, referring to them meant disaster six times. I now imagine a gripe should be included. And it wasn't the police who told me, but Willem did. Not about a gripe. I don't think that crossed his mind, but the other two. What he knew about Napoleon, he liked very much, and as far as that diamond goes …" Her eyes welled up again.

"He wanted to buy it?"

"No way. We don't have that kind of money."

The last five minutes there were spent covering gives and takes about the possibility of catching the murderer. Or murderers.

"What's your opinion, Cath? One or more?"

Her answer was rapid. "The killings are so much alike, I think just one."

"We'll see," Paul said. "In the meantime, if you hear of anything that might be helpful, don't hesitate to call."

They rose and Paul reached into his back pocket for his wallet. He withdrew a business card and handed it to her saying, "Call any time at all."

As they left the house, Vincent asked, "Why didn't you give the others your card?"

"I forgot I had them."

The stop at Jules Mulder's house was a much different affair. His only survivor was a brother, an Episcopal minister who was unmarried and had shared the house with him. No sooner had they been invited in and exchanged introductions than the minister, Koenraad by name, railed on about the circumstances surrounding his brother's death. He rejected the theory as applied to the other victims. His house—outside and in—spoke of that rejection. Paul tried to impress upon him the Baron-Napoleon-gripe connection, but to no avail.

"Especially the gripe bit," the minister said. "If that were the case, I should be one of the suspects because we argued all the time. One of my parishioners showed up at church almost every morning, and he criticized my brother for never showing up at all, even on Christmas."

"Isn't that a gripe?" Paul asked.

"No, it's a statement that spoke in favor of the Lord."

"*Oh boy*," Paul thought. "*We have a religious nut on our hands!*"

"But what about the Blue Baron diamond and Napoleon?" he queried.

"So? Everyone's got an opinion of Napoleon."

"And what about the Baron?"

"All Jules spread around—like a fool—was that if he had the money, he'd buy it. Maybe under those conditions, everybody would."

As for the house, it had a hipped roof, decorative cornices and tall, narrow windows, two of which were covered with stained glass. Its inside resembled a church even more, with narrow pews instead of chairs, a small altar blocking the living room's fireplace, and religious pictures hanging on most walls.

Koenraad was a stout, elderly man with scant hair, wizened features, pock-marked skin, and a weak handshake. He was dressed in jacket, tie and vest, too much for a summer day. And he used an empty corncob pipe to emphasize his points.

"So what's your theory?" Paul asked, already leaning toward an early departure.

"I have none."

"And the tiny diamonds in his wounds?"

"What diamonds?"

"Didn't the police give them to you? And your brother's clothes?"

"I refused to accept a carton they tried to force on me, if that's what you're talking about."

"Were diamonds and clothing in the carton?"

"I have no idea."

Paul decided to go no further, thinking that, all in all, the visit was a waste of time.

Chapter 14

The Park Plaza was within a mile of Koenraad's house and they arrived there in time for the hotel's usual open-dinner serving. After registering for a room and freshening up, they returned to the lobby and headed for an offshoot at its far end. Paul could see tables overloaded with food and, even from a distance, he swore he could not only smell the food but also taste it. They paused at its archway whereupon Paul suddenly held Vincent back.

"What's the matter?" Vincent asked.

"That guy. See him over there?"

He was referring to a large man who was scooping up food in a hurry. He wore dark glasses, glanced around as he went from one table to the next, and he had a mustache!

"Here we go again," Paul whispered. "Let's get out of here!"

They turned around and left quickly and silently.

In their room, Vincent tried to calm Paul down, repeating sentences like, "It may just be a coincidence," and "He's probably harmless."

"All I know," Paul countered, "is that I'm getting tired of all this. The questions, the suspicions, the travel, city after city, back and forth."

"But you've faced things like those for years."

"I know. That's why I'm tiring of it."

It didn't take long for both to be content ordering meals delivered to their door.

After eating, Paul recalled the tiny diamond issue he'd brought up at Koenraad's house and couldn't understand why he'd never broached the subject at any of the other houses. Nor why the relatives hadn't spoken of them. He decided it was finally time to consider fingerprint possibilities. Could they be present on any of the 50 or so diamonds removed from the wounds of six bodies? Were the diamonds definitely left with the families as Officer Webley had indicated? At six autopsies, did the pathologists ever check for prints around the wound sites? If not, were the victims' clothes saved? Should I phone the families to inquire about all this?

It was around 6 p.m. Amsterdam time and a reasonable hour in Angola, Sierra Leone and Belgium. Paul called the families and learned they had all kept the diamonds and articles of clothing.

"They sure were bloody," Angola's Freda Hoek said. "Made me sick for more reasons than one."

"You didn't wash anything, did you?" He was worried not only about washing but, deep down, about the killer wearing gloves.

"No, I just separated the diamonds from the shirts and pants. And nobody from the law has come for them or asked for them."

"I should have. Sorry about that. Anyway, do hold onto them. They may contain fingerprints. Either a police officer or yours truly will be picking them up for testing."

Once in bed and before drifting off to sleep, Paul dwelled briefly on what he had learned in the forensic science domain. He got up, went to his satchel, located the same notes he'd used during the JonBenet Ramsey lecture, and then crawled back into bed. What he wanted to read about was latent fingerprints. As they applied to his current case, doing so wasn't absolutely necessary. It was just that he didn't want to "mess up"—to leave anything to chance.

Vincent was already asleep in the next room and Paul, sitting up in bed, read the following highlights from his notes:

—Forensic technology has improved in the ability to detect latent fingerprints, which are among the most valuable types of physical evidence in criminal investigations. They are accepted by the courts as excellent evidence for personal identification and, if the surfaces on which they have been found are not touched, the prints can last for 40 years.

—There are many chemical and physical methods for detecting and visualizing latent prints at a crime scene. These techniques have expanded the capabilities of investigators at such scenes.

—Fingerprints can be systematically filed using classic fingerprint classification systems and automated identification systems. These files allow for the rapid retrieval of a particular fingerprint card and the arrest of a specific suspect.

—Years ago, police depended on a brush to dust for prints, but now they can use any of 250 chemicals and instrumental techniques to enhance the prints.

—Forensic laboratories can process physical evidence using various methods, depending on the nature of the latent prints. In addition to dusting with powder, techniques include using chemicals such as iodine, ninhydrin reagents, silver nitrate and fluorescent reagents as well as "super glue." Many laboratories are also using advanced technology in instrumentation and illumination to enhance latent prints. These include argo laser, X-ray detection, vacuum coating and various light sources.

—Latent examiners are primarily responsible for inspecting submitted evidence for the presence of latent prints, and then comparing any detected prints with the inked prints of known individuals who may be suspects in a crime. They also provide expert testimony for relevant findings in legal proceedings.

It was the last highlight that caught Paul's attention the most, for he had been asking himself a related question: "Other than establishing that the same person committed the six crimes, what good is a set of prints without having other prints to compare it to—the other prints being those of a possible killer?"

He put the notes aside. His last thought before falling off to sleep was a single word: "Bosnia." It was their final country to visit, and traveling there would begin in the morning.

At 7:00 a.m., Paul stole down to the hotel's small library, looking for its encyclopedic collection. As was done shortly before he visited

Angola, Sierra Leone and Belgium, he wanted to read up on Bosnia-Herzegovina and, especially, the capital city of Sarajevo, which had been the residence of Damir Ademovic, victim number six. He picked out Sarajevo first and read:

> Sarajevo is famous for the products of its carpet weavers and silversmiths, and for its many mosques or Muslim houses of worship. In 1914, Austrian Archduke Francis Ferdinand was assassinated in Sarajevo, an event that precipitated World War I. The city hosted the 1984 Winter Olympics.
>
> From 1946 to 1992, Bosnia-Herzegovina, known informally as Bosnia, was part of the federal state of Yugoslavia. In 1992, it declared independence. Most of the country's ethnic Muslims and Croats supported independence, but most ethnic Serbs did not. After independence was declared, the Serbs, backed by the Yugoslav National Army, began a war against non-Serbs. Serbian forces set up artillery in the hills overlooking Sarajevo and shelled parts of the city. Thousands of people were killed, and many buildings were damaged or destroyed. A cease-fire went into effect in early 1994, but fighting resumed in 1995.
>
> As a country, Bosnia is located in Southeastern Europe on the Balkan

Peninsula. It is bordered by Croatia to the north, west and south; Serbia to the east; Montenegro to the southeast; and the Adriatic Sea to the south. Ethnically, 48 % are considered Bosniaks, 33% Serbs, 15 % Croats and 4% as others. Its population is close to four-million.

After World War II, the country was granted full republic status in the newly formed Socialist Federal Republic of Yugoslavia, but following its dissolution, the country proclaimed independence in 1992. This was followed by the Bosnian War, which lasted until 1995.

Today, the country maintains high literacy, high life expectancy and high educational levels and is one of the most frequently visited countries in the region. It is projected to have the third highest tourism growth rate in the world between 1995 and 2020. It is internationally renowned for its natural beauty and the cultural heritage inherited from six historical civilizations; for its cuisine, winter sports and unique music; and for its architecture and festivals.

When Paul had read enough, he returned to the phrase "inherited from six historical civilizations." He scrutinized it for a moment, dwelling on the word "six", but made nothing further of it.

He knew he'd be visiting Bosnia but, once there, was uncertain of how to proceed other than beginning at Sarajevo's police department headquarters. Over several previous visits, he had bonded with Captain Basil Anagnos who was originally from Greece. The captain would always refer to Greek and Roman influences in establishing The United States as a nation, while Paul would shoot back that, after all these years, Athens still couldn't complete a respectable system of roads. But the overriding reason for their continued friendship was that Anagnos was the most active historian in the entire Baltic region. Paul was first introduced to him by fellow historian Fritz Van Camp. The two had frequently collaborated on important Dutch and Bosnian matters.

By the time Paul returned to the room, Vincent was ready to accompany him during the thousand-mile flight to Butmir Airport in Sarajevo. On the JBCC plane, it took 90 minutes.

PART FOUR

Chapter 15

It was 11 a.m. Captain Anagnos' office was little more than a large collection area for books, trophies and cultural artifacts. Its cluttered floor, desk and a few chairs hardly formed a backdrop for a law enforcement facility, although a cabinet filled with rifles and various police awards on one wall made up for it.

"Thanks for calling ahead," the captain said.

"I did?" Paul said. "Listen, Basil. I do that so often, I can't keep track. But you're welcome."

Basil, of average stature, had an unreadable face with jutting chin, square shoulders and below that, expanding girth. Outwardly, he appeared to be in his fifties and had eyes that focused on his callers as if they were center stage for every second. His uniform was gray-blue, neatly pressed, and had stars across the shoulders. On his left side, three rows of medals could not be missed.

Paul decided to resurrect their ribbing. He looked around and scratched his head. "Well," he said, "I see you haven't cleaned up the place. Aren't you afraid of falling?"

"You never stop, eh? *You* want to clean it? You probably have the time. I'm too busy."

"Maybe *I* could," Vincent quipped, entering the melee.

"No," Paul said. "But let's get down to business. I know you keep in contact with Fritz so you must be aware of the six killings, especially the last one. The poor guy was *from* here."

"Yes, I'm aware of them. Just like all the historians are around here. And they're not all police officers. I've been told that the killer was originally from these parts—our Bosnia, in fact—and then moved away. To where, nobody knows. I heard that the move was after he had a famous Blue Baron diamond stolen from him, which he was going to use as a draw for a business he was planning, and he thought that someone from Sarajevo was responsible. They say he just went berserk."

"That's right," Paul said. "Can you find out more about him when he lived here? If not his name, maybe what he did for a living, or what he planned on doing?"

"I'll try. I do know he helped out in the store for a while ... I mean Damir Adenovic's liquor store. Right after he was the murdered, his wife dissolved the business."

"We'll be going to her house next, and I'll ask her about it."

"Then they say he went on to work for the folks who organized one of our summer festivals, *Bascarsa Nights*. It's a traditional summer festival that takes place each year for the entire month of July. From noon on, it's on our squares and in our theaters. People from all over come for the exhibits and the theater performances. I, myself, go there every year and I do know the Adenovics went regularly. Maybe their killer friend did, too. Maybe he still does—after he resigned his job at the overall festival. It lasted less than a month.

"Hmm, food for thought ... we'll include it on our agenda, such as it is."

"I'll give you the name and number of the person to see. He's its founder and has run the festival for as long as I can remember." The captain reached for an address book in his desk drawer.

"When you find his number," Paul said, "maybe you can get Mrs. Adenovic's address and her first name for me, too."

After Paul was given the phone number and name of the festival's founder—Max Lang—he also received the address and first name of the sixth widow—Dora.

Without urging, the captain phoned her, again expressed the condolences of his entire staff, and indicated that Paul and Vincent would soon call on her as investigators in her husband's death.

He then glanced at a clock on a far wall and said to his two visitors, "Maybe too early for lunch anywhere, but there's great coffee just down the hall."

"No thanks. We'd better leave for Dora's place, and then I'm not sure. The festival maybe. Any place to make my responsibilities more than irresponsible."

"Hey," the captain said. "There you go again. Still the same word master."

"Sorry to cut our visit short, Basil. You've been most helpful, and I hope I can return the favor. Just call."

The meeting ended with the usual handshakes and the captain then led them to the outside entranceway. There, he said, "If I find out anything more about the killer, I'll phone you."

In the taxi taking them to the Adenovic home, Vincent asked, "So what's on the agenda you spoke about back there?"

"Where we're going now; maybe the festival; the lecture in the States; *Invalides*; and I'm thinking of contacting one other person."

"Who's that?"

"Juan Carlos Saltanban over in Gibraltar. He's amazing … simply amazing."

"I agree, but how can he help?"

"With that new invention of his—his 'Synchronous Action Device'—who knows? It helped turn the tide when the world was on the brink. Remember that? Since then, we talk quite often. I'm not saying I'll *definitely* contact him. Depends on how far we get with the other things. In the meantime, I'm getting sick and tired of these interviews. Same questions ... same answers ... or nearly the same. And except for the gripes, what have we learned?" Paul shook his head dejectedly.

"Maybe there's a pattern to the gripes," Vincent said.

"What pattern? I don't see a pattern."

It was Vincent's turn to look dejected.

Curbside before the Adenovic house—more like a mansion—Paul asked the taxi driver to stay put because he expected their stay would not be long.

From their vantage point below many brownstone steps leading up to the front door— Paul estimated at least 50 —taking in the dwelling's entire width required one's head to turn from side to side. Paul recognized its two-story design as Gothic Victorian and featured surrounding porches, lacy trim work and gables topped with finials. All he could compare it to was a home reminiscent of Britain's Middle Ages.

"This from a liquor store?" Paul muttered.

The door opened before he had a chance to knock or ring the bell.

A tall, model-like woman stood before them, smiling, and wearing a yellow silk dress that hugged her hips and shoulders. She was elegant looking and regal in her middle age and, as Paul thought, might still be able to turn the heads of young men. Her face was powdered, perhaps too much for that time of day, and the scent of tantalizing cologne wafted up to them. Her hairline was fashioned sharply under her jaw and brown eyes glistened as she spoke.

"Thank you for being here," she said. "Come right in."

She led them through a foyer with a stone floor, a gently winding staircase and a powder room for guests. Up ahead they could see beautiful paneling, rich fabrics and flower plants everywhere. They bypassed formal living and dining rooms with recessed fans and lighting as they veered off to the right, beyond a set of French doors and through an arch framed by gold-ridged columns. Paul slowed down to run his hand over the columns and then caught up to the others as they approached a through-fireplace that separated a gathering room from a spacious yet cozy-looking study. Plush carpeting covered the floor, furniture was richly upholstered and its walls were peppered with framed prints of seaports, volcanoes and a mixture of luxurious hotel interiors. It was in the study that she signaled them to sit—in a thin triangle with her at the top.

As they did, Vincent whispered to Paul, "Everything about this place is big."

Paul ignored the comment but not Dora. "I heard that," she said, "and I guess everything is. But we worked hard for it."

"Selling liquor?"

"Selling liquor, but also something else."

"Like what?" Paul asked.

"Trips to far-off places. Great profit in that. We did it for about 20 years."

Paul decided not to pursue the subject until later when he would include it in the questions he had in mind. He waited for their host to resume the conversation, but she didn't, instead leaning forward to raise her hemline above uncrossed knees and then to settle in the rounded curves of her womanly bottom. Slowly ... deliberately. Thus far, Paul thought the house, a beautiful woman, worldwide travel arrangements and seductive behavior added up to the backdrop of a prurient Hollywood movie. He couldn't help but wonder if it all had a bearing on why her husband had been murdered.

"So," she said, "you're here ... I'm glad of that ... and I assume you have some questions for me. I've given it a lot of thought and, if it will help bring Danir's murderer to justice, I'm willing to cooperate fully. Some of what I bring out may be embarrassing, but so be it. As I said ... well, you know the rest ... I won't repeat myself."

"I understand, Dora. Oh, I may call you that?"

"Absolutely. Why be formal? That's my name."

"Mine's Paul, and you have no objection to my associate, Vincent here, taking some notes?"

"No, and you both can start now. I'm ready, willing and able." She brushed the tops of her knees as if there were bread crumbs on them.

"First off," Paul said, "you may know all this, but I'll give you a resume of why we were hired." He presented the usual snippets involving six murders; where they took place; the Blue Baron; Napoleon; the sarcophagus; Marlene; Evita; and pirates.

"Yes, I'm familiar with all of it," Dora said. "Especially Marlene."

Paul and Vincent recoiled in unison.

"Marlene? Marlene Kessler?" Paul asked.

"Yes, I used to work for her ... or with her."

"In what capacity?"

"You can't figure it out? She arranged my going along with our travel clients to distant lands."

"How did she fit in exactly?"

"She's been around, as you know, so she set up appointments for me with some men she herself knew ... ah ... quite well. Even with some of our liquor clients who signed up for the traveling. You see, we couldn't advertise it around here because it would ruin our store's reputation. So the ... can I call it like it is?"

Paul nodded and, in the process, nearly choked on mounting saliva.

Vincent began underlining and using asterisks.

"So Marlene was in command of the sex part of it," Dora continued.

Paul pulled back on his shoulders. "Excuse me," he said. "but two questions I hadn't counted on. One—you mentioned reputation. Wouldn't what you were doing leak out back here?"

"No, because my sex partners had reputations to protect also."

"And I suppose the most important question before I get to the ones I'd planned: did Danir know what was going on?"

"One-hundred per cent. He wanted a house like this, the kind of bankroll we have, and I often felt he had his own adventures while I was away."

Paul decided to proceed with the planned questions. "Okay," he began. "Any idea why your husband was killed?"

"Not at all. No, none."

"Did he have any known enemies, especially one or two who had some kind of gripe?"

"Not that I know of. Everybody seemed to like him."

"You're familiar with the connection between the famous diamond and Emperor Napoleon—what I mentioned before?"

"Like I said … *all* of what you mentioned."

"And what was his opinion of Napoleon?"

"Never discussed it."

"What about you?"

"I think he deserves more credit than people give him. At least the people I know."

"Like the ones on your trips?"

"Most of them."

"So if I understand you correctly, among the ones you … let's say … serviced, most didn't think highly of him?"

"Right."

"In other words, a few did."

"You got it," Dora said.

Paul wasn't sure it would or should take place, but then said, "Tell me … not now, but later when I've got some pieces put together … if I should ask you for the names of the people you know who looked upon him favorably, could you do it."

"I think so … yes."

Paul shifted in his chair, the way most would do if they were becoming fatigued. "Now," he said, "we've been told the murderer guy might have worked at the store for a brief period. Is that right?"

"I don't think so or, at least, Danir didn't tell me."

"How long would you typically be out of the country?"

"Depended. Sometimes up to a month."

"So the guy could have worked there during that time and then suddenly quit?"

"Could have. I just don't know."

Paul saw that Vincent was taking fewer notes and that blanched facial skin was showing through Dora's makeup.

"One last question," he said, "and then we'll be on our way. The taxi driver must be going nuts out there. It's about pirates. Do you know any?"

"Yes, some."

"From where?"

"Somalia."

"You know them for the usual reason?"

"The usual."

The visit ended cordially with Paul almost promising they'd have further contact.

During the taxi ride to Hotel Central Sarajevo, where Paul usually stayed, Vincent said, "She didn't seem that upset over losing a husband, did she?"

Paul didn't respond, too busy trying to erase the past scenario from his mind, at least temporarily. Leafing through Vincent's notes didn't help and as he handed them back, he knew full well that eventually he'd have to come to better grips with what had taken place.

Soon after, Vincent said, "She never asked about coffee. I would have liked some."

"Probably doesn't have any in the house. Just some exotic spirits from their store."

"She could have offered something else though, but we wouldn't have wanted to catch the clap."

"Vincent, you're getting too vulgar! Let's just drop it and plow ahead."

Paul's ensuing silence must have concerned Vincent for, within three side streets, he broke it, saying, "Marlene, Evita and now Dora."

The taxi driver's left ear faced straight ahead, his right toward the back. Paul took notice and rather than discuss with Vincent anything that had transpired during the past 15 minutes, he said, "Forward and onward, Vincent. Pure and simple."

Chapter 16

T he hotel was properly named, for it was located in the center of the city, not too far from where they just left. They arrived there at about one p.m.

Unpacking, freshening up in the bathroom and turning down the light covers of their beds, Paul smirked, lay across the bed and addressed the ceiling. "Even this hotel stuff makes me sick," he said. "Checking in, sorting out, tipping, checking out, all the rest of it. Doesn't it you?"

"Yes, I must say. But how else to travel? Goes with the territory. And you didn't include eating. Are we having lunch?"

"Yeah, guess we'd better. Downstairs is good enough."

"Then what? Should we take in the festival?"

"Let's see how we feel. I'd rather take a nap first."

"I'll go along with that," Vincent said. "But I can't see why we have to talk to that founder. What's his name … Max something?"

"Max Lang. I think what the captain was driving at was that maybe Lang might tell us about the guy who worked for him. Maybe he's the killer."

"Who? Lang?"

"No! The guy who worked for him."

"Oh. Sorry. I'm about as tired as you look. Let's get the lunch out of the way, have the nap and then take in the festival."

Paul straightened up and, as if ratcheting up a resolve, said, "Maybe we can even postpone the festival till tomorrow."

"If we attend at all," Vincent said. "Why go in the first place? We don't really need entertainment, do we?"

"It's not *that*. You never know. I read a book once and in it, the villain showed up where the hero happened to be—I think it was in a movie lounge. He took one look at the hero and then beat the hell out of there. Literally ran off."

"So? What did the hero do?"

"Ran after him."

"Did he catch him?"

"No."

"Did he recognize him as the villain?"

"No."

"Then why run after him?"

"I forget exactly, but I think he had a premonition. The point is that you never know what might develop. Anywhere … any time."

They had lunch in a tiny alcove to the side of the registration desk. The food selection wasn't extensive, but they each had a tuna sandwich and lemonade. Usually any food and drink would enliven Paul. Not this time, however. Besides, he was preoccupied with noticing every customer who wasn't necessarily running out of the restaurant, but walking out in a hurry. So was Vincent.

"I wish you hadn't told me about the book you read," Vincent said.

Upstairs again, they napped until five—a full three hours— then agreed to forget the festival until the next day, Thursday.

The square was within walking distance of the hotel. Wearing sweaters, they set out at 11:45 in the morning, an unusually cold one for mid-summer Bosnia. They hoped to be among the first to arrive at the Sarajevo Film Festival, but they were not. The streets were mobbed with men and women in colored vests and leather jackets and even with scarfs guarding their necks. Ticket lines tripled around and they decided not to stand in one but to await some thinning out. In the meantime, they strolled about, bumping into people, and at every street pole, they paused to observe other cinema locations that were visible in every direction.

Paul could never understand why, but he could always tell if an ocean, a lake or a stream was nearby. And even if such waters were dirty or fresh and clean. It depended on the odors that drifted his way. What he smelled here was fresh and clean and he managed to peer out between two theaters to notice a stream winding its way among all the others.

Every so often, they reached a narrow table that contained photographs, announcements and historical summaries under glass. They read part of one summary:

> The first Sarajevo Film festival was held in 1995 at a time when the siege of Sarajevo was still going on. It grew at a remarkable pace and what you see everywhere around you is the most prominent film festival in South-East Europe. It attracts over 100,000 people annually for all programs and for the screening of hundreds of films from 60 different countries. Films are hosted here at the National Theater and screenings take place at the Bosnian Cultural Center off to your left.

As they continued to mosey about, Paul nearly bumped a man off his feet. The man was wearing a woolen hat and had a scarf wrapped around the lower half of his face.

Their eyes met. The man then dug in his heels and ran off.

Paul instinctively ran after him, leaving Vincent behind. *How could this be happening—after I just brought up that book?*

He headed in the direction of the stream, gaining little ground on the man. Finally he lost sight of him within the largest crowd on the square, the one congregated before the Sarajevo Talent Campus. Paul wondered why so many were there until he recalled what a receptionist at the hotel had earlier told him. That the Campus served as an educational and creative platform for up-and-coming young film professionals and that it had come to be revered as the best film training facility in the region.

Several police officers finally converged on Paul, who had no difficulty convincing them that his running was part of a daily health routine.

Once back to where Vincent was sitting on a bench, Paul said, "See what I mean?"

To which Vincent replied, "If he *is* the killer."

"Killer or not, he's one fast hombre. Think he recognized me?"

"I don't know. Everything happened so fast."

In Paul's mind, the incident served as a rejoinder to the question of whether they should spend more time in Bosnia or not. The answer was easy. They would have plenty of time to rest up and relax after arranging for the JBCC plane to fly them to Boston the next day. Paul so looked forward to his second lecture at the Cape Codder Resort and Spa in Hyannis. As was the case in the distraction visit with Maurice at the Lipp, it would serve as another distraction that he sorely needed. He phoned Sylvie and asked her to assure Captain Burns that he would definitely show up.

Chapter 17

O n the way to the States, Paul called Sylvie again.

"You're doing okay?" she asked, not giving him a chance to speak first.

He answered in the affirmative and, although tired of listing experiences, he went ahead once more, condensing some, elaborating on others, and nearly forgetting why he was calling in the first place. He finally remembered.

"Are you coming to the lecture?" he asked.

"What's it about?"

"I thought I'd make it about writing, then forensic science and maybe end up with Jack the Ripper."

"I've heard that talk so many times."

"You don't understand," he said. "It's not to hear me, it's to see me." Paul felt as though he were speaking through the wrong end of a megaphone.

"But I've seen you so many times," she said, laughingly. "No, sorry. I couldn't resist. Just trying to cheer you up, dear."

"It'd take more than *that*. Anyway, since we're both so indefinite, why don't I head for *Invalides* and the sarcophagus right after the lecture? I'm really anxious to give that place the once-over. But after the talk, I'll phone you with how it went."

"Sounds like you're winding down."

"I hope so. I need to."

"But you've made progress? You've got some killer prospects?"

"Some. But I need more information to pin him down."

"Or her."

"Or them."

After a mutual "love you," they hung up and Paul settled back to think about yet another lecture—the one coming up. Their deliveries and how he had gotten used to them was uppermost in his mind. He recollected how weak they were in his earlier years, but since then had grown forceful and positive as they homed in on what was under consideration. Paul understood it all and was not only thankful for his growth, but utilized it for the better as he often referred to it in his opening remarks. He felt that such an approach bonded him with his audience, setting the stage for what was to follow. And he'd never gotten discouraged, for he understood the changeover was not accidental, nor the result of repetition. Rather it was a consequence of his understanding of history. He knew that Alexander lived through the same kind of growth. As did Charlemagne. Even Napoleon, whose history he knew best. All of this lifted him into a position usually reserved for the historical elite.

When Paul and Vincent entered the Cape Codder's conference room, they were met with applause as deafening as it was at the start of the talk there two weeks before. The room was standing-room-only and Captain Burns rushed over to greet them. In the course of some small talk, he said that a gentleman police officer wanted to speak privately with Paul. At the same time, a man appeared at his side. It was the man in the black car! The one who had vanished before Paul's talk was over, last time.

"Good evening, Mr. D'Arneau," he said. "My name is Al Rainford and I work for the Fifth District Detective Bureau. Sorry my wife couldn't make it tonight. What I have to say is that the reason I didn't stay for the end of your talk before was that I suddenly had a more important thing to prevent."

"Oh? Prevent what?" Paul asked.

"Maybe your death."

"My death?" Paul responded, believing the detective was pulling his leg.

"Yes. I'll explain. A guy was up in that balcony that circles around the podium. He was kneeling down behind the spindles. At first I thought he was a photographer. Pretty soon, I think I saw a pistol aimed right at you, but I wasn't sure. I jumped up and couldn't see him any longer. So I left my seat with my wife, told her to stay downstairs while I drew my gun and climbed the only stairs to the balcony. Just a few steps up, I ran into him and he turned out to be a guy I know: Stefan Weiss. He was, and I think still is, the head officer at *Invalides* in Paris. He and some of his staff come down to our lectures every so often and some of us reciprocate."

Paul couldn't believe what he was hearing, much less digest its meaning or know what an intelligent response should be. "So why was the guy up in the balcony in the first place?" he asked.

"I questioned him about it, and he said he'd been having some trouble with his hearing lately and wanted to hear you better."

"Kneeling down?"

"I asked him about that too. He said he didn't want to look conspicuous standing up for everybody to see. So he hid behind the railing."

"And he hadn't drawn a gun at all?"

"Guess not."

"Where is he now?"

"*There* he is, talking with some of our buddies." Rainford gestured for him to come over.

Paul and Weiss expressed pleasure in meeting one another. No further words were exchanged and Weiss disappeared into the crowd.

Paul eyed Rainford skeptically before asking: "Al, is it?"

"Al."

"Al, many thanks for your quick action, but I have a question: why didn't you contact me about the balcony bit?"

"I never made it in time for the end of your talk, and after that, I didn't want to alarm you, especially since I was unsure of the whole thing. And then when I heard you'd soon be coming back here, I just waited it out, thinking it was better to speak to you in person."

"Did you tell Captain Burns about it?"

"No. When all is said and done, I think it was just my imagination."

After Rainford wandered off, Paul wrote down the names Stefan Weiss and Al Rainford in his pad, then related the entire story to Burns and Vincent. Burns pooh-poohed it, but Vincent didn't, saying that after the meal, he'd assume a standing position against one of the side walls.

"Your gun is handy?" Paul asked in an undertone.

"Yes. Yours?"

"Likewise."

Paul was still bugged by two things: the mention of Weiss in the balcony, and the idea of police officers traveling all the way from Paris to Hyannis—and vice-versa—just to hear someone give a lecture. But because he would soon be giving one himself, the bottom line had to be that he couldn't now allow himself to be drawn into a state of shock. If he didn't have to speak just after dinner, he would have felt rattled, but he made light of what he'd been told by saying at the head table— for Vincent's and the captain's benefit—"You know, men, maybe when I speak later, I should do so from the balcony."

Following the meal, Captain Burns gave him a glowing introduction, ending with, "You wanted our man back and here he is!" Applause followed, the type Paul hoped would be repeated or exceeded at the end of his presentation.

Thank you for that, Captain … and thank *you*, ladies and gentlemen. I've been told that some here would like to imitate what I did early in my lecture career. It coincided with my writing career. I've composed some history books but also a few fictional mystery books, so I think I'll lead off with a review of the mysteries I've enjoyed reading the most. There's really some method to this madness because I feel that a progression through the last 176 years may pique your interest in following through with the desire of some of you to compose mystery stories.

This subject's been important to me, just as the act of writing has, so I'll then spend a few minutes on *that*. Next, what forensic science is all about. And finally ... hold your hats ... the Jack the Ripper saga. I'll read a short essay I wrote for the International Association of Crime Writers a while ago. So it's: one—history of the mystery.   Two—recommendations   for writing a mystery novel. Three—the nature of modern-day forensics. And four—Jack the Ripper. Why read that essay? Because so much of it is mired in mystery and myth (As you'll hear me repeat later). And to show that forensics, if available back then, could have easily solved the case.

Paul had begun slightly less relaxed than usual. But by now, he felt totally relaxed and eager to continue. Even spotting Rainford and Weiss in the front row did little to unsettle him.

Edgar Alan Poe—1840—176 years ago. He was the first legitimate mystery writer. There had been plenty of true crime stories written before his time, but never any mysteries. See, to have a mystery, there must be two ingredients: a crime must be committed. Murder, of course, is the ultimate. And then there must be some effort at detection, whether by a police officer or a detective or some other kind of memorable character. Poe's memorable character was a detective named C. Auguste Dupin. Then there was a gap of about 50 years and along comes Sir Arthur Conan Doyle and his Sherlock Holmes mystery series. Memorable character? Obviously, Sherlock Holmes. Well, these two authors and their memorable characters represented the *Dawning Age* of mystery writing.

Then onto the *Golden Age* of the 30s, 40s, 50s and thereabouts, with such giants as Agatha Christie and memorable characters, Hercule Perot and Jane Marple; Earle Stanley Gardner with Perry Mason, portrayed on television and in the movies by Raymond Burr; Ellery Queen ... this one is kinda complicated. Manfred Lee and Frederic Danney didn't like the sounds of their names so they wrote under the pseudonym of Ellery Queen—and they named their memorable character? You guessed it: Ellery Queen. As I said, complicated. Finally in this group we have Rex Stout and his character, Nero Wolfe.

Now, I should have said it before, but all these authors and their works are my favorites. There are plenty more, as you know. Okay … while this was going on, a number of authors individually and collectively believed that the prior group was, yes, important in blazing a trail, but that they were old hat and rather stiff and stodgy. So this new group wrote in a less constrictive style. Chief among them and my favorite mystery writer of all time is Dashiell Hammett, who wrote the *Maltese Falcon* starring Humphrey Bogart and Mary Astor. Also Peter Lorre and Sydney Greenstreet. Memorable character? Tough guy Sam Spade. Hammett also wrote the *Thin Man* series starring William Powell, Myrna Loy and the dog, Asta. Besides Hammett were Raymond Chandler starring Philip Marlowe and Mickey Spillane starring Mike Hammer.

And that brings us to the current crop of excellent writers, one as good as the next. Like Mary Higgins Clark, Elmore Leonard, Sue Grafton, Robert Parker, Michael Palmer, Robin Cook, Patricia Cornwell, Michael Creighton, Ann Perry, P.D. James.

Paul looked around to be sure no one had fallen asleep. Hardly. And one could hear not merely a pin dropping, but even a speck of thread.

Next, a few recommendations for writing a mystery novel and, unlike what I first covered, I'll be consulting notes for a good portion of this so as to keep it straight. First of all, do remember my saying that in mysteries, a crime must be committed. Well, it must be a significant one, and the solution must not be stumbled upon. In other words, elaborate.

Make your hero sweat. If he or she isn't in trouble, your book is. And don't tailor your challenges to your hero's strengths. Real growth through the course of a novel occurs when overcoming weaknesses, not just utilizing strengths alone.

Introduce the villain early. And spend as much time on your villain's motives as your hero's. Remember, the hero reacts to the villain—or potential villain—which means that such a person is the motor of the plot. It's a balancing act, really.

Suspects are cheap, so have enough. Five or six is a good number. If the crime is murder, pick a victim worth killing. This means several people should have motive, opportunity and means.

Let your characters impact the plot, not the reverse. Put another way: novels should be character driven. P equals CMWEO. That's "plot equals characters messing with each other." And don't force your characters to act out of character simply to further plot ends.

Paul was surprised—and happy—to see that more and more attendees began taking notes. By now, he guessed about half the audience.

Have your characters **act**, not be acted upon. In this regard, nobody loves a villain, and there are reasons why protagonists are called heroes. Basically, they're loved. Villains are not. The well-known axiom, "Show, don't tell," enters the picture here. In other words, show the protagonist deserving love—and the villain not deserving it. Not just telling about it.

Now, paragraph frequently in tense scenes. If not overused, one-sentence paragraphs can pack a lot of punch. And shorten chapters for effect. Witness the late Robert Parker's writings.

Avoid generics—go for specifics. Don't let characters walk streets and drive cars. They should walk along Park Avenue looking for their Hondas. Mysteries revolve around details.

Use proper official procedures. Don't trade plot convenience for reader credibility. Do your homework.

Pile on the puzzles. One isn't enough—subplots can give your mystery texture and provide a counterpoint for the main plot. In other words, they set it off by contrast.

Remember, everyone has something to hide. A seemingly straightforward murder can uncover an entire spider's web of suspicion. In your book, everybody who would have killed the victim is a little guilty—the killer just got there first.

Disguise rather than withhold crucial information. All clues discovered by the hero must be made available to the reader. In other words, fair play. Readers need to see the pivotal clues without realizing what they're reading. Solving a mystery using withheld information is cheating the reader.

Use plot twists to add surprise. But not out of the blue. A plot twist works best if it's an unexpected change on the elements already presented in the plot. For instance, an investigation eventually determines that a victim's companion on an ocean cruise was not the person listed on a confirmation document, but someone else.

Finally, spend some time on forensic science because it's current and extremely valuable. So I've touched on:

—mystery requirements
—the victim
—the hero
—the villain
—suspects
—other characters
—show, don't tell
—suspense seeds
—shortened paragraphs and chapters in tense scenes
—specifics, not generics
—added puzzles
—disguised information
—plot twists
—forensic science

And that's what I have to say about writing mysteries—for those of you who are thinking of doing so. From the looks of it out there, I'd say quite a number. Well, I hope I didn't go too fast.

Now on to the nature of forensic science. What is it? The most concise definition I could put together is that it's the application of biological, chemical and physical sciences to matters involving the law. I'd like to begin this topic with a quote from Sir Arthur Conan Doyle's first novel, *A Study In Scarlet*—written in 1887. Many feel he had considerable influence in implementing techniques in serology, in fingerprinting, in firearm identification, in questioned document analysis, and in blood spatter analysis. He was writing about these long before the scientific community knew much about them. Here's what he wrote:

"I've found it. I've found it," he shouted to my companion, running toward us with a test tube in his hand. "I have found a reagent which is precipitated by hemoglobin and by nothing else ... Why, man, it is the most practical medico-legal discovery for years. Don't you see that it gives us an infallible test for blood stains? Now, this appears to act well whether the blood is old or new. Had this test been invented, there are hundreds of men now walking the earth who would long ago have paid the penalty for their crimes. A man is suspected of a crime months after it has been committed. His clothes are examined and stains discovered upon them. Are they blood stains, or rust stains, or fruit stains, or what are they? That's a question that has puzzled many an expert, and why? Because there was no reliable test. Now we have the Sherlock Holmes test, and there will no longer be any difficulty."

Simply amazing! That was 129 years ago!

With respect to forensic science in general, there was a time when it and criminalistics were considered one and the same. But not any more. It's sort of an oxymoron, but the science has both expanded and contracted. Expanded in terms of bringing more disciplines under its umbrella, and contracted in terms of specialization—much like what's taken place in medicine.

So … imagine forensic science as an open umbrella. Down its center is a pole—its core. This is still criminalistics or criminology. What is it? It deals with crime scenes. With the recognition, collection, identification, preservation and interpretation of physical evidence at crime scenes. It also includes crime scene reconstruction. And at the bottom of that center pole are offshoots or subdivisions like:

—DNA analysis
—latent fingerprint analysis
—questions document analysis such as ransom notes
—ballistics
—drug analysis

—voice analysis

—data banks for fingerprints, DNA, tool marks, tire marks, and spent shells

—artificial intelligence involving crime mapping (which is how crime spreads), criminal profiling, crime scene reasoning and logic (that is, getting into the mind of a criminal)

Now then, off to the side of this center pole are many other poles that are squeezed into my depiction. In fact, you name any field, put the word "forensic" in front of it, and it now exists:

—forensic medicine

—forensic odontology (dentistry)

—forensic anthropology (skeletal remains)

—forensic entomology (life cycle of insects to pinpoint time of death)

—forensic engineering

—forensic nursing

—forensic photography

—forensic accounting, for heaven's sake (blue collar crime)

Paul felt a trickle of sweat between his shoulder blades but he knew it was "good" sweat that came from thinking far, wide and fast about a familiar subject and then citing its essentials.

"Finis for forensic science," he said, sipping from a glass of water. "I'll wind up with the essay I wrote about Jack the Ripper." He separated two or three pages from his notes and read:

The time: a nine-week period in the fall of 1888, sometimes referred to as *"The Autumn of Terror"*.

The place: the Whitechapel district of London. That was the east end. Where the slums were. Where prostitutes flourished.

Jack the Ripper: Few names in history are as instantly recognizable. Fewer still evoke such vivid images: noisy courts and alleys, cabs and gaslights, swirling fog, prostitutes decked out in the tawdriest of finery, the shrill cry of newsboys—and silent, cruel death personified in the cape-shrouded figure of a faceless prowler of the night, armed with a long knife and a Gladstone bag.

And his identity is still unknown—although there's hardly a year in the 128 since, when a new brainstorm doesn't emerge. When experts don't continue to speculate. I won't dwell on the many aspects of this saga—it would take a full day. But I'll list a few:

1—the homicides themselves, at least five, usually with terrible brutalization.

2—the victims, all prostitutes, usually older, and with alcohol problems.

3—the investigation—intense, prolonged.

4—the endless theories.

5—the abundance of graffiti.

6—the varied letters and postcards—some considered sent by the killer, but most considered hoaxes.

7—the suspects: a mad doctor, a professional butcher, a deranged mid-wife, a mysterious lodger, even a member of royalty.

Actually, so much of the Ripper is mired in mystery and myth. And with the passage of time, much can get (1) exaggerated, (2) embellished upon, or (3) otherwise distorted.

I have a simple way of viewing such things: "The older the story, the more grains of salt it should be taken with."

But here goes. It's not very long—quite concise, in fact. I'll just devote the next couple of pages to why the Ripper continues to be discussed. To give you a sense of what it was all about.

I must emphasize, first and foremost, that Jack the Ripper created the myth representing the evil archetype of the more modem serial killer. This isn't to say that the whole story is a myth—just that the story has been one of mythical proportions. But by today's standards of crime, Jack the Ripper would barely make international headlines.

—the murder of five prostitutes in a slum swarming with criminals?

—just one more violent creep satisfying his perverted needs?

—no, hardly anyone would be incensed over the fate of those five prostitutes as were the respectable families and friends of the pretty college students who were Ted Bundy's victims. At least 30, here in the United States.

Unfortunately, we've become a society numbed by horrible crimes inflicted upon many innocent victims—especially in the last dozen years or so.

Why then, are there still stories and songs and operas and movies and a never-ending stream of books about this one Victorian criminal?

Why are there many Ripperologists and no Bundyologists?

Why is the Ripper story as popular today as it was in Victorian London?

For two main reasons: First, because Jack the Ripper represents the classic whodunit. The story has a terrifying, almost supernatural quality. It's been said that he came out of the fog, killed violently by slashing a throat from ear to ear, and quickly disappeared without a trace. And after his last victim was found, he vanished from the face of the earth. Forever.

But over time, much has been distorted. And that brings us to the second reason for its continued fascination: misimparbarism. In spite of their barbarism, the murders represent a real-life mystery from the era of Sherlock Holmes—the late 1880s—the bygone, romantic era of high Victorian society, with gaslights and swirling London fog, as I've said.

But get this! Not one single killing took place on a foggy night! Not one single killing had any real relationship to Victorian splendor.

Plus—of all possible coincidences, at the same time these murders were occurring, guess what was thrilling audiences across town at the Lyceum Theater, in the fashionable West End?

The Strange Case of Dr. Jekyll and Mr. Hyde!

Together—these two things—a classic whodunit and the Jekyll and Hyde coincidence gave many people their first awareness of the potential for inherent evil in so-called normal individuals.

Finally, I'll abruptly end this brief essay with—first—no hint of who I think the killer was, because I haven't the slightest clue.

And second—with the unabashed claim that if DNA and the New Genetics—that is, modem forensic science—had been available back then, the mystery would have been cracked in short order.

But just imagine—if that had been the case, we probably wouldn't have such a lasting melodrama, would we?

And that concludes my talk. I thank you for the opportunity to give it and for your attention.

There was complete and utter silence. All the police officers and guests appeared stunned over Jekyll and Hyde. But then, as Paul sat down, the room shook with cheers and stomping. A standing ovation followed and Paul followed suit, clapping less gingerly but with hands held high and circling the room.

The captain offered his congratulations; several attendees converged on Paul to do the same, including Rainford and Weiss; and even Vincent, who came over from his lookout position.

Giving the talk had worked wonders for Paul. As hoped for, it was an interlude that gave his mind a rest from the demands of his assignment, and not even an early inward eye on the balcony scene had made a lasting impression.

He and Vincent waved as they left the conference room and once in the sedan that had driven them there, Paul phoned Sylvie and gave her a verbal thumbs-up sign. He also mentioned Stefan Weiss. He indicated that they should be arriving at *Hôtel des Invalides* early the next morning, Paris time, and wished it wouldn't be a Saturday. But she stated that for such iconic buildings within the complex, all days of the week were the same.

Chapter 18

On the plane, Paul asked himself, "Has there ever been a flight when I didn't read up on the place I was going except for Sierra Leone and Belgium— but in a distracted state of mind at the time?" Accordingly, he leafed through the Paris file in his satchel, located *Les Invalides* and read:

> **Hôtel des Invalides** is a complex of buildings in the 7th arrondissement of Paris, containing museums and monuments, all relating to the military history of France, as well as a hospital and a retirement home for war veterans. Included is the **Dôme des Invalides**, a large former church that contains the burial tomb for Napoleon Bonaparte.

The tomb is often referred to as his sarcophagus. It consists of a casket within and a scrolled cover, and made of red porphyry, a variety of granite, rising high toward a double cupola and pendentives of the dome. An elaborate bronze door leading to the sarcophagus is flanked by two colossal bronze figures that bear symbols of imperial power on a cushion: the crown, the sword, the globe and the hand of justice.

At the base of the sarcophagus is a multicolored, star-shaped mosaic recalling Napoleon's eight most famous triumphs: Rivoli, the Pyramids, Marengo, Austerlitz, Lena, Friedland, Wagram, and Moskowa. And circling around are twelve winged statues in Carrara marble, symbolizing victory.

Within various recesses, at two levels and not far from the sarcophagus, are several paintings that evoke themes defined during the reign of Louis XIV; that celebrate the Catholic religion; that show angels holding the symbols of the religious and warrior monarchy; and that highlight a shield with the coat of arms of France.

They checked into a local hotel but spent little time there. Unpacking and settling down would have to wait, for they opted to leave for *Invalides* without delay.

They entered the dome cautiously and without invitation. It appeared that scores of visitors were trying to lower their echoing comments.

It didn't take long for a young man to approach them saying, "Welcome, gentlemen. I'm Chester Knight, the assistant police officer here. Do look around, but please don't touch anything." His smile looked sincere.

He was neatly dressed in a gray police uniform with a revolver at his waist and a large medallion pinned to his left chest. It contained a photograph of Napoleon. Paul thought he looked too young, too short and too thin for a cop—maybe even too handsome. But he said nothing about it for fear of offending him.

"Thank you, officer, and don't worry—we'll keep our hands to ourselves. I'm Paul D'Arneau and this is Vincent Broussard. We're from the United States."

"You are? That's where I'm originally from. New Jersey."

"Well, I'll be," Vincent said.

"Maybe that means we can level with you better," Paul said. "We're here not on a sightseeing tour—I've done that before—but for something more specific."

"How can I help?" Knight asked.

Paul then spoke of his assignment in somewhat vague terms, but he did refer to the six murders.

"The specific reason for our visit," he said, "is that we want to check out one of the paintings here, the one that was recently replaced. Is there one?"

Knight's expression became dour, his age doubling. "Yes, there is," he said.

"I take it you didn't like the idea," Paul said.

"You're right."

"Who did the replacement?"

"My boss, Officer Weiss."

"Who gave him the authority to do so?"

"Himself. More and more he rules the roost around here. To be honest with you, I've resented it, and that's the reason I turned in my resignation. I have a day to go."

Knight walked them over to a soft-cushioned bench. Paul and Vincent sat down but the officer remained standing. "I'd join you," he said, "but it wouldn't look right to all those other people." He ran his hands over his abdomen as if in pain and then continued: "You know, if you hadn't told me you were from America, I wouldn't be talking this way. But somehow you look trustworthy."

"We try to be," Paul said, "and I wouldn't worry about it. Now ... is Officer Weiss around?"

"Yes, he is. Over there. The other one in uniform. He's looking this way. In fact, I think this is where he's headed."

Paul and Vincent rose and when Weiss reached them, Paul shook his hand saying, "Well, we meet again, officer."

"Again?" Weiss said.

"Yeah, we met last night. At my lecture in Hyannis."

"Sorry, I don't remember being there."

He rushed off like a scorpion in retreat.

Paul and Vincent looked at each other in disbelief. Paul scratched his head and addressed Knight. "Is he alright? We chatted just last night and he doesn't remember?"

"That's the way he's been lately. Ever since he replaced that painting. He says he'll do one thing and then does another. He breaks promises. He's late for all staff meetings, if he shows up at all. He orders me around as if I'm a kindergartner. 'Do this. Do that. Hurry up.' And he leaves himself wide open. Didn't used to."

"Wide open?"

"About many things—serious and not so serious. It's gotten to the point where I can't put stock in anything he says."

"Good reasons for you to leave," Paul said.

"You better believe it. All in all, I feel that ever since I began working in this place, I've been cut off from the outside world—except for the newspaper I get at home."

"You said 'I'. You're not married then?"

"No, not yet, but I'm going with a wonderful woman. She's in college to become a police officer, too."

"Where's that?"

"John Jay College of Criminal Justice in New York City. That's where I went for my Master's degree. She's also working on one."

"Is it out of bounds to ask where you live?"

"Not at all. In a complex near the Eiffel Tower."

"I see. Fairly nearby."

The more Paul heard, the more he thought Knight sounded like a true-blue American and the more he felt comfortable with him. "By the way," he said, "May we call you Chester?"

"No, make it Chet."

"Okay. And we're Paul and Vincent."

There was a letup in their conversation until Paul said, "So why did you leave New Jersey for here?"

"I heard there was an opening so I jumped at it. Boy did I miss the boat."

"When did you start?"

"About six months ago."

"Weiss seemed okay then?"

"Yes, but he began to change about two months ago."

Paul was drawn to some quick arithmetic. *That was about when the murders started!*

"What else can you say about him?" Paul asked.

"He always seemed to bring up his admiration for Napoleon and for diamonds. It was as though that was the reason he took the job here. Why diamonds would attract him, I can't say, except I do know that Napoleon loved them. And on the side, Weiss became an expert at diamond cutting because that's what his parents did in Denmark."

"And you say Weiss replaced the painting … but why?" By now, Paul was beginning to feel that any question could be raised, and that soon it would be safe to open up, himself.

"He told me he had some things to write down and wanted them stored in a location that was not only safe but also symbolic."

Paul flashed a troubled look.

"Symbolic of what?" Chet added. "I have no idea. Symbolic of some kind of power? But in the course of doing so, he accidentally tore the painting that was there—so he put up a new one."

"Did he ever tell you what was stored behind the new one?"

"Yes, and I didn't have to yank it out of him. The nature of his crazy thinking again. He said it was a two-fold message, as he called it. One concerned the diamond cutting process, and the other was the secret to making replicas of a so-called Blue Baron diamond by an acquaintance of his. He said he didn't like that person making replicas because it made him more powerful, and Weiss didn't like that. He also bragged about ordering many henchmen who used pearl-handled guns to work on behalf of that acquaintance."

"Did he say who the acquaintance was?"

"No, and I didn't ask because I knew what might have happened."

"What?"

"Retribution."

Chet shrugged and made a helpless gesture. "I'm sorry," he said. "I really don't understand it all. What I understand though is that when a guy becomes unhinged, he's liable to say anything. Even *do* anything."

"Hmm, unhinged is a good way to express it. Any idea why he became that way?"

"He said there were six atrocities but didn't elaborate. That he helped the other guy six times— I assumed with the atrocities. And that he was promised payment for doing so, but the guy reneged. They argued and argued and eventually Weiss stole the diamond."

The three of them stood near the bench. Ten minutes before, Paul had an urge to sit again but what with the surprise from Weiss and the information gleaned from Chet, the urge was completely gone. Not gone, however, was what he'd earlier told himself might become a possibility. It was time to open up, even though he had never shared this kind of sensitive information before ... particularly with someone he had just met. But he was confident there would be no collusion between Chet and Weiss, and that was enough to base his decision on. In addition, he felt he owed it to him, in view of what Chet had shared.

Paul explained that the atrocities referred to the six murders; that they had relevance to a Blue Baron diamond; and that the utterance of Napoleon's name was significant.

Chet arched an eyebrow when the murders were mentioned, so high that Paul believed that the officer would never digest what was to follow.

"Do you know anything about the Blue Baron?" Paul asked.

"Oh, yes ... I forgot to mention that it's the name of the diamond that Weiss stole."

"How did he know where it was kept?"

"Apparently he somehow pried it out of him, but I don't know how."

"Looks that way. Now the question of all questions. Do you think Weiss was capable of assisting in murders?"

"In his state of mind? I'd have to say that I believe so, but not in the actual killings—only in identifying those to be murdered and in providing their addresses."

Paul sat down, not caring whether the others would join him, but they did.

He thought: *How fortuitous. Why didn't I come here sooner? The damn traveling and the interviews to accumulate suspects. The trip to Argentina to question Marlene. The Pink House and Evita's diamond box. The trip to The Hague to hear about Milosevic. Bothering Fabio, the tons of police captains and all the histarians. The convenience luncheons. All the reviews I took time to read: Napoleon, Angola, Bosnia, piracy, latent fingerprints. I'm still planning to read up on the Rock though. Its magnificence and my ordeal on it deserve the attention. But other than that, no more reviews unless absolutely necessary.*

He worded it that way to Vincent, who was in agreement.

Paul resumed his thinking: *Then there was the Sarajevo film festival to chase wildly after a suspicious-looking man. Meeting with Guy Martin. The two lectures and the Maurice distraction to calm my nerves. All of this, and one of the most likely suspects is right here. What a waste! Now all we need to do is identify that acquaintance."*

During that interval, Paul noticed that Chet was paying more attention than ever before. *It was time.*

"Chet," he said. "I have something to discuss with you, but only in private. Would you by any chance have an office where Vincent and I could meet with you?"

"Yes. Up in the gallery. If you can call it an office. It's really just a small room with very little in it. But we can go there."

"Now?"

"Sure … now."

They retreated toward a room that overlooked Napoleon's sarcophagus. Before entering, Paul paused to gaze down and made a sign-of-the-cross over his lips.

Inside, the room appeared just as Chet had portrayed it. No windows. Simple desk. Bare coffee table. Two ordinary floor lamps. Plain wooden chairs. Small cot. No books or magazines in sight. A shelf containing riffraff plus a row of audio tapes and recorder."

"Sorry about this," Chet said, "but it's what they gave me. Doesn't ruin our talking though, so what's on your mind?"

Each sat stiffly around the coffee table.

"It's time to do something I've been putting off until the right moment … and this is the moment," Paul said. "As soon as possible, we should visit with a man named Juan Carlos Saltanban in Gibraltar. He's a good friend of ours and two years ago he developed a certain device that helped a team of ours prevent a Japanese-led sarin attack on the whole world. We talk every so often and he's indicated that he's improved on what the device can do. He explains it this way: that it used to work in an inanimate mode—the 'what, where and when" capability, he calls it. And now he's added an animate mode—'tracking human conversation.' It's kind of a location and monitoring component. Well, maybe the improved version can help us out. This unusual man ... he was once president of Radonia, a tiny country in South America, but now has his own big-time business at the foot of the Rock of Gibraltar."

Chet focused alternately between Paul's eyes and mouth. He skipped the Radonia and Gibraltar references and asked Paul to clarify "location and monitoring".

"He can identify a phone caller and monitor his or her conversation, but he can't yet identify the other party—the one at the receiving end."

"You mean if I called you, he can tell who I am but not you?"

"That's it, but he's working on the next part of it. And I'm wondering, Chet, would you be willing to come with us to confer with him? I value your judgment. Right, Vincent?"

"That we do."

"I'd be more than happy to," Chet replied. "Whatever helps."

"Excellent!" Paul exclaimed. "Yeah, excellent! We can fly there in the morning. Now then, I see you have some audio stuff up on that shelf. Does the recorder work?"

"Yes. Music and my cot. That's how I survive in the few breaks I have here."

"Well, I happen to have a CD of an interview with Saltanban."

"Naturally, it's in that overstuffed satchel of his," Vincent said. "He calls it his 'miniature library'."

"Overstuffed to everybody but me. Wish I could carry along *more* material. But that's another issue. For now, I'd like to play the recording for you. It might give you some insight about Juan Carlos before you meet him. And I must level with you, Chet. What I meant before by your 'input' has to do with collaborating with him in a certain way. A *close* way. But I'll explain that to you later."

Chet took the recorder down as Paul removed the CD from his satchel.

"This isn't exactly short but is very interesting and informative every time I hear it. And two other things: I'm the questioner—and—see if his speaking without contractions irritates you as much as it does us."

Juan Carlos, tell me first about the advice you gave your son.

Ah, my beloved son, Luis. Here is what I said to him. You have received a legacy that I began many years before you were born. Handle it wisely with the skills you inherited from me.

And be careful of ordinary politicians. When they speak, do you not for a moment know they are politicians? Certain corporations try to buy election results and the beneficiaries are favored politicians. If a "good' politician must be good in the art of compromise, then truth, honesty and loyalty are compromised.

Contrariwise, if a politician shuns lies, deception and betrayal, he or she can achieve only ordinary status—a stranger to the inner circle and unable to accomplish much. Thus the stuff of politics is such that it attracts scoundrels or eventually creates them.

But none of this pertains to you, Luis. You are different. You are my son. Be my son. Be strong. The struggle will take years, if not generations. But you will have the temperament, individuality and determination of your father.

Good advice. Now, before you went into politics, you were in communications. How did you get started?

It is a long story. As a boy, I was always taking radios apart. Later I became an aficionado of the history of communications. Even in high school, I knew that would be my field someday, and in the meantime, I read all I could about the history.

I do not mean to bore you, but at the beginning, the first form of long distance contact was what? Smoke signals.

Then some people called the Sumerians developed the first known system of writing; the Romans started the first newspaper; and the English introduced the first pencil.

Next, the French developed photographs and three of your Americans—Morse, Bell and Edison—invented the telegraph, the telephone and the phonograph. The radio came in there somewhere and I think a Canadian was involved.

Paul and Vincent were paying attention as if they hadn't heard any of it before. And Chet was wide-eyed after lying back on his cot, arms supporting his head.

As I have said—although I did not give a date—Samuel Morse invented the telegraph in the early 19th century. He later developed the Morse Code. The telegraph was a very important instrument during your Civil War for both the press and the armies of both sides. And it helped at your stock exchange and at your railroads.

What can I say about the telephone? Bell discovered it in the late 19th century. And you know, a funny thing. One never thinks of it, but at the beginning, there were no switchboards. They came during the next year. Then dial phones, service between countries, and the technology I am most interested in: commercial satellites. Think of these as relay stations. But I have said enough about these devices. I am afraid I ramble once I begin. Some other time perhaps, I might discuss the radio and the phonograph.

And so you see, it is all related—all these forms—and all the countries, somehow many of them wanted to—how do you say—wanted to get into the act.

Anyway, we are now up to the things I am most interested in. They are plans about telecommunications. Advanced telecommunications.

Meaning what?

My plans about telecommunications? Forgive me but I shall become more technical. Bell Laboratories discovered the transistor; Xerox the copier; and Corning Glass the first optical fiber that could be used for long-range communication. Fiber optics uses a laser to send signals through glass or plastic.

The transistor, which replaced the vacuum tube, is a tiny device that controls the flow of electric current in TV sets, radios, computers and ... there I go again. I am sorry.

I spoke about satellites already. Telstar is a satellite that was launched in early 1960. It relayed telephone calls, television shows and other commications between your country and Europe.

My country dealt with fiber optics and satellites primarily, but I have recently become interested in cybernetics. In point of fact, three months ago, I completed a book on the subject, and I am anxiously awaiting word from the publisher. I would like to advance knowledge about how information is transmitted by the control mechanism of machines and the nervous system of living things.

Like animals?

Yes, animals. Humans. Yes, anything living. But I believe I have rambled on too long. You asked me the time and I made you a watch!

Nonsense. That was most informative. A couple last questions though. What about computers? Where do you think they're taking us?

I am concerned. The Internet with its encrypted messages can be such a tool of secrecy that crime of every kind will become electronic and will take place in an instant once the decision is made. Drug operations, fraud, embezzlement, prostitution, blackmail, government conspiracies, military coups, murder. Much is possible now, but it can get worse. In the matter of terrorism, for example.

And even in business or education or government work, face-to-face meetings may no longer occur, and I think much will be lost there. It is really a sword with a double edge. Email. The Internet—an Information Super-Highway, but one that is filled with—what are they called? Potholes?

It is the secrecy that is my worry. Split second. Cheap. Yes, cyberspace is good but can become evil. I am afraid this hemisphere and perhaps the whole planet has an analogue intelligence surrounded by a digital threat. That is how I see it.

Now back to cybernetics. It is a science that deals with how humans and machines can be similar and how controls can work in both.

Would you mind explaining that again?

Controls or feedback. I believe that eventually we can build a machine to imitate human behavior and even to identify the voices of selected people at great distances. But, until that time, we should concentrate on controlling that behavior.

What's the title of your book?

Mechanization: The Alternative to Cloning.

Sounds very ambitious.

It is really not. My premise is that machines should be able to accomplish more than the simple mechanization of work. After all, it is humans who are designing the machines.

And?

And through feedback or control, the machines can become more human. I have chapters in there on institutional conditioning, on biofeedback in medicine, and even on transcendental meditation.

There. Now we're talking.

Now we are talking?

Yes, that's what I'm interested in. Transcendental meditation. TM. In the medical field, there're so many patients, say, with chronic infection who also have high blood pressure or asthma or migraines. If they can only be taught to deal more effectively with their autonomic functions, it would be a blessing. I know there are centers for this sort of thing—stress reduction techniques and the like—and they usually do a good job. But not always. Do you think it can be improved upon?

Yes, I do.

Could you come speak to our state medical society one of these days?

It would be my pleasure. If I could help someone, I would be honored.

"Whew! That's some background, and he really knows his stuff," Chet said, looking for Paul's response.

"Indeed."

"What did you think about his lack of contractions?" Vincent asked.

Chet answered with a straight face: "Sorry, I did not notice that, or maybe I did not want to. Do not tell me that you noticed. But I would not mind because it would not make any difference. Do you not see it that way?"

As Paul slid the CD back into his satchel, he and the other two were still chuckling. More importantly, he was even more convinced that Chet was the right person to accompany them to Gibraltar. They agreed to leave at seven in the morning.

Once back at the hotel, Paul phoned Saltanban and was assured that he looked forward to seeing them and to highlight the added features of his new device. He would make reservations for them at the Caleta Palace Hotel.

Paul never mentioned a thing about his assignment or about the device's possible role in a successful conclusion.

Then, before calling it a day—more like a week—Vincent said, "Paul, my friend, you said back there that you'd like to go over one more review ... the one about the Rock. I read it before, but wouldn't mind doing it again. After the encyclopedic part, I liked the part where you reminisced about your captivity there. The business of 'spelunking' and 'caving' and 'paradoxical undressing'. Your description of things is so real, so graphic. I can't resist it, Paul. And now's a perfect time to read it again. Do you still have both parts?"

"Of course. The two combined into one is one of my favorites. You read it first and then I will too."

Paul located it easily and gave it to Vincent. It took him ten minutes to read before he handed it back to Paul:

> The Rock of Gibraltar is a limestone promontory of the British overseas territory of Gibraltar. The territory has a population of about thirty-thousand. Most residents are descended from Italian, Maltese, Portuguese and Spanish settlers. Others are descended from British military personnel who were formally stationed there. Almost all inhabitants live in apartments in the town of Gibraltar, and the workers are primarily employed by its government, by dockyards or in jobs related to the tourist industry.

As for the Rock itself, it is nearly 1,400 feet high and is located off the southwestern tip of Europe on the Iberian Peninsula. It is considered crown property of the United Kingdom, forms a peninsula that juts out into the Strait of Gibraltar and borders Spain. Occupying nearly all of Gibraltar's 2.3 square miles, most of its uppermost area is covered by a nature reserve where about 250 Barbary macaques reside. These animals—the only wild population of monkeys in Europe—along with a labyrinthine network of tunnels—attract numerous tourists every year. The underground tunnels are known as the Galleries and the Great Siege Tunnels.

These underground tunnels have a unique history. They were first dug in the late seventeen-hundreds. The British commander wanted to create the potential for cannon fire upon Spanish batteries in the area below the north face of the Rock. The siege lasted about four years and during that span, the British constructed six such embrasures and mounted four cannons.

The so-called Galleries were constructed later on. Comprised of an entire system of halls, passages and embrasures measuring nearly a thousand feet long, they too are a popular tourist attraction. From that location, visitors are able to view the Bay of Gibraltar, the isthmus and Spain itself.

All told, the Rock contains over one-hundred caves. The most prominent and the most visited is St. Michael's Cave, situated halfway up the western slope of the Rock. Within it is another area called Cathedral Cave, once thought to be bottomless and therefore an underground link to Africa. This has never been substantiated. Cathedral Cave now serves frequently as an auditorium for concerts, ballet and drama presentations. The beauty of its crystallized surroundings draws raves from its numerous attendees. They are particularly drawn to a centuries-old stalagmite that became so heavy, it dropped and landed on its side at the far end of the chamber.

From a military standpoint, it was fortified by over thirty-thousand British soldiers and sailors during WWII, thus playing a key role in the defense of shipping routes in the Mediterranean. In 1942, during the war, the Allies launched an attack from Gibraltar against German and Italian forces in North Africa. And as recently as 1997, it was revealed that Britain had concocted a secret plan to hide servicemen in the Rock's tunnels in case the Germans captured it. It was named "Operation Tracer" and had the radio capability to report all enemy movement. A six-man team remained undercover for over two years before they were disbanded and returned to civilian life.

Such a history of sieges and military action is responsible for the popular saying "solid as the Rock of Gibraltar." Technically speaking, it is not based on the solidity of the Rock itself, rather on the action and dedication of the servicemen assigned to it.

The following is my recollection of being held captive there. I've tried to be as accurate and complete as possible. In fact, I cannot help but remember most details. Only the dialogue may be off somewhat. Where I wasn't certain of the exact words spoken, however, I've inserted my best memory of them:

I heard a knock on my door, rose and opened it. Four men, all tall, brawny and overly mustached, pushed me aside and burst into the room. Three of them kept their hands in their jacket pockets. The fourth identified himself as Tony and spoke fluent English. He barked at me: "Now don't say a word or make a silly move and you won't get hurt. Just come with us. Once again, no questions asked. You understand?"

My first inclination was to ask a simple question or two. Wouldn't you? Maybe they had come to the wrong room.

I felt my heart pounding, but still took a chance with a single word.

"None?" I asked.

"None. Just walk along with us to our van. We're driving up the Rock to a place I'm sure you've never seen. We'll keep you there until we receive further instructions. It might take awhile."

I felt fortunate I wasn't hammered by one of them for asking the single word.

Two of them grabbed me, one on each side, and the five men, closely aligned, headed down the corridor toward the back exit.

It wasn't long before the van reached the Cathedral Cave. A single taxi was ahead of us, followed by a line of others.

I was glad I wasn't blindfolded, but reasoned that my captors didn't want to alert anyone as to what was happening.

On the way, I gawked at the apes, wishing they were human enough to understand the situation and go for help.

When they reached the fallen stalagmite, the van pulled off to the side. The men waited for all the taxis to pass before squeezing out and leading me through a rusty gate that was hidden by the stalagmite. They remained outside as I stooped to enter, and I offered no resistance for fear of being roughed up. Tony then closed the door and said something like, "We'll be in touch." He then locked the gate—I don't remember how.

Right about then was when I wondered who ordered this ... this imprisonment.

Through the bars, I said, "Now that I'm locked up, may I go ahead and speak?"

"Be my guest," was Tony's answer.

"Have you ever been in here?" I asked him. You see, I was already planning an escape based on my knowledge of worldwide caves and tunnels and I figured the less they knew about the layout there, the better.

"No," Tony said. He laughed and laughed, saying, "but I hear it's cool and cozy." I wished I had him alone.

Then they all disappeared. To where, I don't know.

From here on in, what I can describe has to do with what I faced without anyone trying to stop me. It wasn't easy, believe me, but I made it or I wouldn't be here to tell about it.

Just inside the gate, I strained to maintain my balance on craggy footing. I turned in a circle without feeling threatened, probably because I recognized the enclosure as some kind of anteroom to a cave tunnel. I reinforced my confidence by reviewing my many days of "caving", which included negotiating pitches, squeezes and—God help us—water holes, water streams and dirty ponds. But that was a long time ago. I stopped once I hit age 40, but before that, I'd regularly undertaken it for sheer enjoyment or for exploration as in mountaineering or diving.

This is where the term "spelunking" comes in. It refers to exploring caves as a hobby. For years I had a bumper sticker that read: "Cavers rescue spelunkers."

I can still see the lack of illumination and it got worse the farther I got, inches at a time. Soon I was enveloped in a montage of giant crystals and rock formations. I could identify most of them: the obvious stalactites and stalagmites, helictites, cave pearls and baconstrips formed from what were called dripstones and soda straws. What I could make out in the dim light, despite my experience, looked like an alien world. But the footing got better, I stumbled only once, and it became time to explore. I made out a higher landing beyond the overhang of a jagged side precipice. I found a gnarled length of wood propped against it and used it to claw my way upward, but it was a tedious process. Very tedious. Twice, I remember, I stepped on a rocky projection that split off, but I somehow managed to keep from falling by grasping others. I knew that if I did fall, it would have been curtains. And then, halfway up I guessed I was at the point of no return and wondered why in hell I'd begun the climb in the first place. Talk about being caught between a rock and a hard place! But somehow I plowed ahead, or rather, *up,* and once on top, the light was dimmer and the air was chillier. Frigid, really. I was out of breath and coughing. What a feeling! I fell to my knees, then leaned back against—you guessed it—a large rock. I can still feel the clouds of dust worsening my cough. I was sure I had only minutes to live, and how does one feel when he's about to die? Does his whole life flash before him? Is that just an illusion or does it really happen? How would we know anyway? The person dies!

But instead of screaming which I should have done, I ran through some of my earlier days when I volunteered to search for missing mountain climbers and was introduced to a phenomenon I'll never forget: "paradoxical undressing". It's what happens to some people when they're exposed to extremely cold temperatures over a long period of time. Hypothermia and it could lead to death. These poor souls are found undressed because they experience hallucinations and feelings of warmth. Their bodies are found in a protected location— under a bed, behind a couch, behind a boulder. I'm told that the theory is that this behavior is due to a primitive brain stem reflex of burrowing, as can be seen in hibernating animals. But it wasn't happening to me. I wouldn't let it. I recall checking my arms and found them cold, but not any different from when I was outside on a snowy night.

I squinted straight ahead and was able to make out a sloping tunnel that began far off. Not *too* far though—maybe a golfer's delight of 95 yards.

This time, I was convinced I could see a sliver of light. I pulled myself up and headed in that direction, brushing away spider webs and dodging bats flying by. As I trudged and trudged over uneven footing and still craved food— a sure sign that my ordeal hadn't wiped away my appetite—I thought how favorable it was that Tony and his goons hadn't passed beyond the gate with me. If they had, I might not have had the opportunity to climb the precipice, as perilous as it was.

The physical patterns of a whole host of caves crossed my mind as I moved along. Ones that I was familiar with: branchwork, angular network, anastomotic, spongework, ramiform. I knew, first-hand, that most were composed of carbonate rock, but even when I reached the start of the tunnel, I couldn't decide what I'd be traversing.

One thing was clear, however: I'd be dealing with a steady stream of water, possibly with tributaries that would converge from the sides, feeding into the main current. How high the current would get suddenly became my main concern. I rolled up my pants to my knees.

Three-quarters along, I made out a gate ahead, similar to the one I'd entered before and prayed it wasn't locked.

Throughout the entire length of the tunnel, the water came no higher than my ankles and, reaching its end, the gate opened easily. I walked out, pivoted around and gave the exit of the tunnel a sarcastic salute.

"Great as usual, isn't it?" Vincent asked. "Now where are we in current life?"

"Immersed in a brain-teaser just as complicated."

Chapter 19

The flight to Gibraltar took less than two hours.
Shortly after takeoff, Paul called Sylvie. He told her about Chet and about the Weiss incident at the lecture. She took it all in and then warned, "Careful of him."

"Who? Chet?"

"No. Weiss. He sounds dangerous."

Addressing Chet, Paul said, "We must decide on a way to have Weiss and his acquaintance speak to each other. By phone and at a given time. Any ideas?"

"I'm tossing around possibilities," Chet replied. "Maybe your Saltanban friend has improved further on his device and can help even more."

Paul had been thinking about leveling with him during the entire trip and, as they approached Gib Airport, he did so. "Chet," he said, "I don't know whether or not you suspected it, but much of my feeding you all those questions was ... well ... you were being interviewed."

"I realized it."

"You did? How come?"

"The training at John Jay College. They taught us how to secretly interview someone and also how to recognize *being* interviewed."

"Of course! I remember it all. I should have known."

"And did I get a passing grade from you, Paul?"

"Chet ... you wouldn't be with us now if you didn't."

After checking in at the hotel, they walked toward Saltanban's office complex on Catalan Bay, only a stone's throw from the hotel. In reality, the bay was a tiny village nestled on the eastern side of the Rock. The office was at the far end of linked buildings, their green exteriors glistening in the early morning light. When Paul had been there twice before—four years ago, and two years before that—he remembered each time being taken aback by the faded exterior of the buildings, but now they appeared updated, even reconstructed. They came upon a large ebony door, opened it and walked onto a balcony that Paul vividly recalled.

From their vantage point, nothing had changed except there was more to see. The number of rooms below had once again increased—to perhaps a hundred or more. He estimated that each room measured about 30-feet square. They were interconnecting, had open entryways and were occupied by male and female workers, busy at computers, and never looking up to acknowledge their presence. The backside of the workers' upper garments bore an emblem depicting a black silhouette of the Rock.

The contents of each room were no different: a beech-colored swivel chair with a waterfall seat edge and contoured backrest; teak side tables that held computers, printers and copying machines; a gigantic shredder; and, in the center, an elongated table with a glass top below which a powder-coated steel frame rested on numerous cubic pillars.

Paul was impressed and saw that Vincent and Chet were too. He whispered to them, "The same kind of work bays, only more. The same kind of work force, only larger. They act like robots, only faster. *Is he somehow controlling them with his Synchronous Action Device?*"

A narrow corridor forked around from front to back. As they walked along, Paul looked up and noticed something new: combined visual and auditory units attached near the ceiling, a set of them at roughly 50-foot intervals.

Suddenly, a tall, hefty man approached them. It was Saltanban.

"I saw and heard all that," he said with a smile. "And no, I'm not controlling my workers. They control themselves and maybe could control *me*."

He shook Paul's hand first, then Vincent's and Chet's. He shook Paul's again saying, "I am so happy to see you. I know Vincent from before, but not your other associate here."

"This is Chet Knight, Juan—a police officer from the *Invalides* in Paris. He's part of our team now."

"Team? Team for what? But wait. Let us go to my studio."

He led them down the corridor, its left wall composed of solid glass. The view was that of plush meadowland and attractive hillside homes.

They reached a triangle of rooms. Paul recalled that the one on the far right was Juan's studio and the center one was for storage. But now, the left one had a steel beam across its front with a padlock at the end.

Paul pointed to it. "Your synchronous room, I take it?" he said.

"Yes, that is what it is. I shall show you in a minute. But in case your new man here is wondering—what you saw on your way in is our administrative wing. Down the hall from here ... out back ... that is our production wing. It is much bigger. It has more people. And everything we do here has to do with electronics and fiber optics."

Inside the studio were several work tables that appeared to be collapsing from pile upon pile of papers, maps and assorted paraphernalia. Around one table, there was just enough room for an ordinary desk and four chairs, which Saltanban arranged in a circle. They sat as if on cue and crossed their legs the same way.

Everything about him looked the same, only older and a little more stooped. His goatee and head of hair were now almost totally gray. Approaching 60 and well over six-feet tall, he wore square, wire-rimmed glasses. He was dressed in a blue shirt with matching striped tie, and dark trousers that reached slightly above the waist in an obvious attempt to cover a slight paunch.

On each finger was the usual gold signet ring, a "J" in script on the left and a "C" on the right. Once again, and for Chet's benefit, Paul asked why there was not simply a "JC" on one ring. And the response was as anticipated: "No, no. These are for 'Juan Carlos.' Your way is reserved for one who is more important than I."

Saltanban uncrossed his legs and leaned forward. "So," he said, "other than because of our friendship, what brings you here, Paul?"

"It's got to do with my new assignment."

Paul then outlined it—six murders and all—and gave specifics regarding the need to identify the recipient of a phone call. He referred to what had been explained to him by Chet: that a Stefan Weiss feared retribution if he were to inform anyone of his acquaintance's name. If Weiss agreed to cooperate at all, he said, it would only be by tapping into a phone call.

"Incidentally," Paul said. "I don't know if this has any bearing, but he failed to recognize me after we chatted just a few hours before."

"Remember though," Chet said, "He's been losing his mind in all sorts of ways."

"But why would Mr. Weiss cooperate in the first place?" Saltanban asked.

"I'll let Chet take over from here."

"Weiss assisted Mr. X in some way," Chet said, moving a hand from side to side to emphasize the names. "Not in the commission of the murders, but in helping set them up. From a legal standpoint, if we can assure him of leniency if he phones the killer at a set time, he might be willing to go along with it."

"And that is where my device comes in, I take it."

"Correct," Paul intervened.

"And I'd be willing to make the pitch to Weiss," Chet added.

Saltanban got up, went to a window and signaled the others to join him.

"See that Dragon Tree over there?" he said. "If I chop it down, it no longer has a name. If I chop down Mr. X, he no longer can murder. And gentlemen, I am willing to chop down Mr. X."

Paul had witnessed such dramatics before. And with them came success.

"Much appreciated, Juan," he said. "And now, the improved device. May we see it, or would you prefer to elaborate on the new 'animate mode' first?

"Either way, but let me repeat one part of what I said to you during our last phone conversation. The animate mode is what I label 'tracking human conversation', but as of now, it cannot identify the person being called. The caller can be identified, no matter the distance—even if he or she is thousands of miles away from where I have the device set up. But as I now think about it, what good is identifying the caller? We already know who he is because we asked him to be that person in the first place."

They had already returned to their chairs when Saltanban began the elaboration, and when it ended, each of the others reacted the same way: arms folded across the chest, head moving from side to side.

"But," he added, "all is not lost. I have an idea. I cannot identify the receiver, but I *can* record his voice, and that is what I will be doing. So two things can come of it. One is that his voice might be circulated around and someone might recognize it. And two, if certain things can be brought up in the conversation—and Chet or you, Paul, can rehearse this—things that point to one, and only one, person ... well, you know what I mean. Then we have the identification. For example, there may be one thing he said he did once. And then he says he also did another thing. And on and on, if necessary. In the end, if doing every one of those things applies to only one person, we have him. But the timing would have to be just right. The 'things' cannot be said in a row. That's why I mentioned 'rehearsal'. In the meantime, I am still working on improving the device."

A brief "who speaks next" silence filled the room until Paul said, "Under the circumstances, it's what we're forced to do, but it makes good sense, Juan. Let's go ahead."

Then Chet kicked in: "As soon as we return to *Invalides*, I'll meet with Weiss, and we'll know soon enough if we can proceed."

"And to be sure we get the timing right, you will notify me about how you make out with him?"

"Yes, as soon as it's over, and I hope it's good news."

"Now the device, Juan," Vincent said. "I'm anxious to hear what Chet thinks."

During their walk to the far left room, Saltanban said, "I am sorry if you have already heard this, but my device can now identify most individuals legitimately employed throughout the world, but not those who move frantically from one job to the next."

He led them to the padlocked room and lifted away the steel beam. Inside, on a table no larger than two-feet square, was a box with a sliding front panel and a golden metal handle at the top.

"I'd forgotten how small it is," Paul said, "and even what the inside looks like. You won't believe this, Chet. Are the gadgets the same, Juan?"

"The same, but there are more of them."

He slid the panel aside to reveal row upon row of miniature screws, nuts, bolts, washers, switches, wires, clips, hooks, ball-bearings, dials, pins, needles, levers, knobs, eyelets, tubing, brads, springs, clasps, staples, chains, hoses, sprockets, cables, valves, blades, belts, bushings, camshafts, drills, rods, adhesives, sealants, grommets, pumps, compressors, wheels, shafts, hammers, buttons, fasteners, discs, latches, braces, tacks, hinges, cords, locks, and plugs.

The sight rocked Chet back on his heels.

Saltanban slid the panel back and said, "Again, forgive me if I repeat myself to you, Paul and Vincent, but for Chet here, I must say that my invention is entirely unique. Space is the key. Commercialization of space is changing at a rapid rate. What do I mean by commercialization in this context? Well, nothing more than satellite radio, satellite television and satellite navigation systems.

"The word 'artificial' is often tied to the word 'satellite' to differentiate it from natural satellites, which are objects that orbit the planet. The earth's moon, for example, is a natural satellite.

"So we have satellites and cybernetics. My new system—which is the one I will call upon for our joint challenge—puts them together, and I call it 'satelnetics'. In other words, it has features of both. And I shall not speak about it any further. Suffice it to say that I shall be able to locate and identify the caller, but the callee ... *there*, I have coined a new word ... the callee is a different story."

At the ebony door, Paul indicated he was due for a decent nap and would take one on the way back to Paris. "I travel so much," he said, "that sometimes I'm too tired to get up from a chair to take a nap in bed." They shared a loud laugh.

Saltanban had accompanied them to the door, wished them well and said he would await a future call, either to begin the process or to delay it until further notice.

"You say his full name is Stefan Weiss? Is that not so?"

Paul answered him while nudging Chet with his elbow: "Yes, it's so ... I mean, yes, *it is so* ... sorry about that, Juan ... and thank you."

Chapter 20

T he only thing keeping Paul from having that nap
was his uncertainty about Weiss' response. The
three agreed the response was critical.

"I wonder how it will go with him," Paul
said.

Chet responded: "In his state of mind, it
could probably go either way. 'Yes, I'll do it' or
'up yours'."

Again, it was only a two-hour flight. They
reached the dome just before two.

Weiss was wandering around aimlessly.
They marched right up to him and Chet said, "I'm
here to pick up the rest of my belongings and to ask
you something, Stefan."

Paul joined in: "We know what you meant
by 'atrocities' when you spoke about them. And if

you don't like the word that it stands for, we won't use it."

Paul figured that such a statement might soften Weiss up.

"So if you assisted in them, we can arrange for your immunity, but your end of the bargain would be to phone your acquaintance at a specified time."

"For what?"

"To arrest him. To get him off the streets. To confine him to prison and insure that he wouldn't be able to speak to the outside world."

The last part of Paul's answer—speaking to the outside world— was given in view of Weiss' possible fear of retribution. Retribution in the form of a pearl-handled gun being fired his way. Then, in the most basic language, Paul explained the role of Saltanban.

Weiss jumped at the proposition as if he needed no further convincing. "When and where?" he asked with the kind of gusto usually reserved for winners of Olympic Gold.

"As soon as possible and from right here," Paul said quickly, fearing he'd hear a change of heart. "Can you easily reach him?"

"Yes."

"What will you talk about?"

"I'll think of something. Maybe he wouldn't talk for long unless I brought up the Blue Baron diamond. I'm not even sure he knows that I stole it, but I'll tell him I did. *That'll* make the bastard keep talking."

Chapter 21

For Paul, time was passing with little relationship to other events, other than calling Sylvie. Such was his eagerness to inform Juan of what had just transpired.

First he phoned *him* with the news and was greeted with a stoic, "Good, it is as I thought, and I shall get on it. Do not worry ... I shall keep you informed."

Do not worry? He's got to be kidding.

"You'll start now?" Paul asked. "In other words, Weiss can call him right away?"

"Right away. It takes me only a few minutes to activate my device. Takes a little more to interpret what I monitor."

Then the call to Sylvie.

"I've been very anxious to hear how you made out," she said.

"Just fine. Juan was very cooperative and he'll implement the plan."

"So Weiss agreed to it?"

"Hundred per cent. It was so easy ... so easy."

The three men decided on an early dinner just outside *Invalides*. Paul couldn't believe that he had no further interest in locating the painting, much less what was behind it.

Before dessert was served, he felt his smartphone vibrating. Saltanban was on the line.

"I cannot tell you who the callee was," he said, "but he had a funny way of talking."

"Funny?"

"Yes. He used words like 'whilst' and 'amongst'. He used them a lot. When Weiss asked him why, he said, "My upbringing.""

"What were the words again?" Paul asked.

"'Whilst' and 'amongst'."

Paul's own words stalled in his mouth. *Whilst. Amongst. The English upbringing. We have our man!*

He harked back to when he first met Police Officer George Webley in Amsterdam. He remembered the way he spoke.

Paul explained everything to Juan, thanked him in glowing terms and indicated he'd be kept informed of any and all legal proceedings. He then stuttered some as he told Vincent and Chet what Juan had said.

"So it's Webley. Now what?" Paul asked.

"I'll notify my law enforcement friends in Amsterdam," Chet said. "They'll round him up and arrest him."

"On what charge?" Vincent asked.

"Multiple murders."

"But what if he claims there's not enough evidence?" Vincent shot back.

"Aha ... that's where Weiss comes in again! We'll see him before we leave here and tell him how valuable he was in helping Saltanban. When Weiss hears of the claim of not enough evidence, he can come to the rescue by naming our man."

Paul's words were stronger now: "So we'll have ... one ... those words of his. How many people speak that way? And ... two ... Weiss' testimony. Together, that should be plenty."

There were many loose ends left within Paul's assignment, but he couldn't have cared less about them. To him, the most important takeaway was three-fold: the capture of a mass murderer; the preservation of a respect for Napoleon; and the recovery of the Blue Baron diamond.

The murderer was at hand and a certain respect for Napoleon was secure in Paul's mind. But of singular importance, the Blue Baron returned to a leading position atop the world's

diamond industry. Monetary worth notwithstanding, what still counted heavily among most
admirers was its *mystique*, a feature that was
augmented by a combination of factors: majesty in
size and brilliance; unique beauty; and to those in
the know, a rare mix of chemical composition and
crystalline structure that made its color a
translucent blue.

EPILOGUE

Some issues must be addressed:

Officer George Webley was found guilty on six counts of murder and sentenced to life in prison without parole.

Except for murdering, he had patterned his life after Napoleon's.

He wanted Weiss as an accomplice because of the *Invalides* connection and the serving as his representative there.

He killed Otto Bleeker because he believed he might replace him as Amsterdam's top police official.

Paul soon informed Leon Cassell of the facts surrounding Webley's identification. Leon would remain Chairman of *Gens de Veritas*.

Chet Knight and Al Rainford would likely work for him in the future.

Stefan Weiss was pardoned of all criminal activity, regained his sanity and continued with his duties at *Invalides*.

He allowed no one to examine the back of the replaced painting.

Evita's diamond box was left behind at the Pink House.

Marlene expanded her already widespread ventures.

Juan Carlos Saltanban pursued further potential of his device.

The Blue Baron diamond was donated to the Smithsonian Institution.

Sylvie was promoted to Chief Administrator at the Woods Hole Oceanographic Institute.

And Paul confined all future treasure hunting to the continental United States, nullifying any consideration of international travel.

Author Jerry Labriola, M.D.

Biography

As an author and crime analyst, Jerry Labriola, M.D. lectures extensively on mystery and true crime issues, and conducts workshops on the elements of the novel. After his first exposure to forensic pathology while serving in the U.S. Navy, he practiced medicine for 35 years and was an Assistant Professor at the University of Connecticut Medical School. A Yale graduate and former Chief of Staff at a major teaching hospital, he also served as State Senator and ran for Lt. Governor and Governor of Connecticut as well as the United State Senate.

He is the author of 13 mystery novels. He is also coauthor with renowned forensic scientist, Dr. Henry Lee, of four books dealing with forensic science.

Dr. Labriola writes full-time and is a member of the Mystery Writers of America and of the International Association of Crime Writers.